# EMBAIXADOR

# EMBAIXADOR

## MARCUS JOHN BELTRAN

"TWO FRIENDS. TWO WORLDS.
TWO CHOICES. ONE ANSWER ..."

**Lytenial Books**

lytenialbooks.com
ISBN: 978-1-7346820-0-7 : Paperback
ISBN: 978-1-7346820-1-4 : Ebook

*To my children and entire family, I dedicate this book.*

*To those I had the honor of sharing a part of my life with, and to everyone present or now away,*

*I dedicate this story.*

*As a young thirteen-year-old a question came to me. A question that has been asked from the beginning of time. Is it to an end? Or merely a beginning? Thirty-two years later, this answer, my message, is told.*

*"I've chased it my entire life, determined to catch it and never could. Now, I know it was never to be caught. And so, I ran with it. It, was my imagination."*

-MARCUS JOHN BELTRAN

*"Behold, in that vision clouds and a mist invited me; agitated stars and flashes of lightning impelled and pressed me forwards, while winds in the vision assisted my flight, accelerating my progress."*

-ENOCH

*"It was the day I passed, and I lived to tell it."*

- CALEB JOHN MCCRAY

# 1

## THE GOOD LIFE

IT WAS A nice, warm day, in spite of the rain in the forecast. Large, full clouds filled the sky, as birds chirped and soared overhead. The grass was green and lush with bright, colorful flowers. Sunlight shone through the leaves in the distance. There I found myself sitting up against the same big oak tree I've known since I was a child. It's at this very spot I would always come, just to get away.

"Damn! The time!" I yelled, jumping up. "It's okay, mommas, I'm fine," I told my dog, Nalla. All I remember telling myself last was to stay awake, no matter what. Tiana, my wife, made it clear she finally found the right person we'd been looking for. I, however, had my doubts.

It was when Tiana gave me that look and said, "I'm telling you, Caleb, this person is the one. And it's time to reveal this. It's time to show him," that she convinced me. Tiana ran into this man at Tublin's, the local grocery store the week before, and she told me his name was Steven Riley Franks. He goes by Riley and he was the owner of the barber shop in town. She said he was going through severe personal life issues. They were the exact issues I had gone through.

As Tiana talked with Steven that day, she told him I had a touching story she strongly felt would help him. Steven was excited to hear it, and Tiana gave me his phone number. I talked to Steven that evening, and he was elated. We got to know each other more and I could tell he was going through a lot.

Steven said he would really like to hear what I had to share, and he asked if I knew of a place with no distractions. I told him I did.

And so that's when we agreed to meet. Right here, at this very tree, which I call Good Ol' Faithful. This beautiful and quiet place has one of the largest trees around, off Highway 77. And yet, somehow, it's only noticed by some.

As Nalla and I waited, I began to wonder if Steven would show. He called and said something had come up, and apologized for having to reschedule our meeting. Before we hung up, I made sure he knew just how special my story was. I told him it was special, because it had to do with him.

He was both baffled and intrigued, and couldn't wait to hear it. I had put everything on hold for him, even sleep. Sleep, however, was no longer my friend.

I'm looking forward to sharing my experience with my new friend, Steven. I know how vital it was for him to hear it. If only he knew who he really is and what he's really capable of.

Until then, I'm going to share a little about myself and what I've finally discovered.

My name is Caleb John McCray. Like all of us, I made some mistakes in my life, which started at a young age. It was the consequence of one of those mistakes, however, that cost me everything. I became desperate. Since then, the ongoing flashbacks of that decision and dreadful morning have become more frequent. I'm forced to relive it, every day.

If only I didn't answer that phone that evening. If only I had taken the time to look and see it all coming.

It all started with a good life. I had everything an everyday working American guy needed. I was twenty-five years old, with a gorgeous and loyal wife named Tiana Emily McCray, who was twenty-three. And of course, my precious, little, six-year-old girl, Taylor Marie McCray. When my little girl came into my life, she became my entire world. Tiana and Taylor made me the happiest husband and father alive.

Along with my wife and daughter, I had a great job as a young executive at a local bank here in San Diego: Wayland Financial. I drove a nice car, had a big house, with money in the bank, and practically debt-free. If I didn't have it all, I was close. I truly had a wonderful life.

I've always considered myself a pretty decent person who enjoyed life just as much as the next guy. My family was very close. My mother, Katy McCray, is the strongest woman I know and my rock. My precious sister Kristen Lilly Marie, resilient, as the blows of life roll off like water. I also had the loving guidance of my aunt Lydia and godmother Gayle. And, my wonderful cousins Robin, and Elaine Frankie, who has been there when others could not.

I was pretty well taken care of. One would think with all these strong and amazing women in my life I would stay out of trouble. And, of course, my coworker, Jason Bell, and his wife Marisa. Jay would do anything for me, at any time. In fact, he has been there for everyone, it seems. He is really a brother to me, and my best friend.

My friends and family were a big part of my life. To have a little boy along with Taylor would complete me in every way. Tiana felt the same way, and had worked on expanding our family. After trying for over a year for a baby boy, we had no luck, and started to get concerned. I was reminded, as I often am, of my mother's words, how she told me not to believe in luck, only blessings.

So I tried hard to remain positive. Soon, though, our worst nightmare was confirmed. After one of Tiana's checkups, the doctor told my wife she could not have any more children.

We were devastated. Even after hearing this, Tiana never gave up hope. I wish I could say the same.

And my dad, Marc McCray. I'm very close to him; in fact, he is my hero. My father was a mailman. A damn good one. He loved his job and lived to help others. Even at age six, I never forgot what he always told me. He said, "Stay away from the crowds and trends." It wasn't until much later I knew what he meant.

I can hear my dad even now, asking me as a child, "Hey sport, you want to walk with me to the corner store for some ice cream?" Of course, I would always smile back, nodding yes with excitement.

Just being with my dad made me feel so good. I can recall one time, walking back from that little corner store, eating my ice cream with one hand, while holding my dad's hand with the other. I would always look up at my father. On that particular day, as I looked up at him, the sun glare was so bright I could barely see his face. All I could see was part of his mouth as he looked down at me and smiled. It was as if he was reassuring me. He patted my head. I smiled from ear to ear as I held his hand tighter. Oh, how I miss those days.

My father saved my mother and me, along with another woman and a store clerk, from a robber. Like it was yesterday, I remember everything, from the gunman's face and raspy voice to the black clown ski mask he wore. For some reason, he had a patch covering one of his eyes over the mask. He looked right at me as he lifted his mask just over his mouth and gave the scariest grin I had ever seen.

Out of nowhere I heard *bang! bang!* The gunman fired two

shots into the ceiling as he continued threatening to kill the clerk and all of us. "Give me the fucking money, now! No bullshit! I will kill all your asses dead! I don't give a fuck!"

My dad kept trying to calm him down, telling him it was going to be okay.

"It doesn't have to be like this, please," my dad pleaded with the gunman.

"Shut your ass up!" the gunman replied. I could hear the other woman there, praying softly to herself. "Don't bother, bitch, cuz ain't no one listening to that shit. Even if they are, there ain't no prayer that's gonna save you this day…" the gunman said with an evil chuckle.

"Whack!" The gunman pistol-whipped the woman in the face, knocking her to the ground. The second the man pointed the gun at my mom and me, my father lunged at the gunman, pummeling him to the ground. "My God, please, no!" my mother screamed in horror as my dad desperately wrestled the robber for the gun. I remember hearing thuds and grunts as they struggled and fought. Panic and confusion were all around. "Katy…run! Run!" dad shouted.

Mom grabbed me up onto her shoulder while running to the exit with the other two women. While my mother ran with me on her shoulder, I faced backwards and I never took my eyes off my dad. I can't even tell you what that did to me to see my father on top of that man as they struggled like that.

The punches and kicks continued as we headed to the exit. Just as we got outside, I saw the robber flip my dad over and hit him over and over. With my arm stretched toward my father, I screamed as loud as I could, "Daddy!" while Mom ran through the front doors to the outside.

I know my mother never meant for me to see that in such a state of panic. No one thinks how to react or choose how you should in that kind of moment. Just as we turned the corner outside, I heard three gunshots. I looked up at my mother as she screamed, "Oh God, no!" She covered her face, crying.

I hugged and held my mother tightly, with tears falling down my cheeks. Police and the ambulance arrived and rushed my dad to the hospital. We found out that two of those shots hit my dad, and later that day, at the hospital, he died. It was as if mom already knew. Her face said it all. The masked robber was never caught.

My father saved us all that day. I miss you, Dad, so much. To lose a father at six years old, to lose any parent that young, does something to a person.

A deep anger has grown in me ever since that day. An anger that's been growing stronger as I got older. I have always questioned mom and everyone else. I even questioned and asked God, Why? Why did my Father have to die and for me to see it as a child?

Dad never deserved that! He would help anyone at any time, and he always put family and others first, no matter what Mom always said.

Mom shut down for many years after what happened, and hardly spoke. Outside of her regular job at Bailey's Fabrics as a seamstress, she also had to work nights at High-Mart, the twenty-four-hour grocer, as a clerk, to make ends meet. My mom would drop me off at my granny's in the morning, and I would not see her until late that night. Through it all, she remained positive and loving. We both would have our moments. Whenever I would walk in the room, she would quickly hide her tears, assuring me she was okay. Knowing she was not, I would always hug and comfort her.

And whenever some days got hard for me, I would again ask my mother, why did it have to be dad? She would always say, "He was called. It was just his time to go home, son. God has a plan for all of us."

I soon realized Mom's answer was not acceptable to me. *Oh, really?* I now thought. *So God did this, then? So that's Dad's reward for being the best father and person ever?*

He saved his family and others, and in return, he got that? No! Fuck that!

Hate began to consume me.

Growing up with all of this in me, from when I was a young boy, took a toll that would lead to other extracurricular activities in school and out. So, to cope and distract me from it all, or maybe just for fun, I decided to turn my hate and frustrations to all the bullies and troublemakers in the school.

Who did they all come to for help to take care of matters? Me.

I wasn't that big of a guy; however, I was just the right size to deliver a big-time ass-kicking to anyone. In the ninth grade I had seniors on the run. Trust me, they wanted no part of me. I never lost a fight, during all of my schooling years, except for one. But we won't talk about that cheap shot piece of shit.

And so, after many fights throughout high school, my reputation preceded me and I quickly became known as the beat-down artist.

However, in my junior year I got bored. I wanted more. I was done with these high school kids. I wanted to expand and see how good I really was, physically and intellectually, and had an idea. I added outside punks to my list, beating down grown men's asses.

Going big and official was my goal, and so I combined my two best skills: strong business mindset and fighting.

I loved both. And with that, I officially got in the beatdown-for-hire business; BeatDown Inc. was born.

I did rather well making a quick buck, and I do mean quick. On a bad day with no breakfast, maybe it was a five-minute job. And as far as the money for each case, I got upwards of $250 per head, and roughly three cases a week, which wasn't bad for a seventeen-year-old.

My mother eventually found out, and didn't take it well. I

gave her a hard time as I tried to wiggle my way out of it all with lies and excuses.

I essentially began to put my own mother last and didn't care. I have always hated myself for that. So, growing up was pretty tough. Although, most of us have had rough childhoods and upbringings. This may have been why I've always felt different as a young boy. It seemed that no matter what, I could never fit in with anyone, or with anything, and I never knew why. I was never liked. I was feared.

Through the many years, I kept asking my family and other's why I lost my father. I would only hear many different answers. No. I knew there had to be more. This and many other questions grew. I began to wonder if there really was a God, and ask, why would any God allow such things to happen?

And if there isn't a God, who decides who lives and dies at certain times? In fact, what is the purpose of life itself, and our very existence? All these questions have tormented me ever since. What was the point of living, just to die? I was determined to discover exactly what that was.

Now, into adulthood, I've had strange, unexplainable experiences. Of all these oddities, was a dream that has really bothered me. We all have them, of course. However, there are some dreams you never forget. For a while now I have had this one bizarre dream of a young boy in the middle of nowhere. It has truly affected me ever since. I would awake breathing heavily and bothered inside. There was something about that kid. I was unable to explain it to Tiana.

As I continued to experience all of this, I started to wonder if there was something wrong with me.

I knew it was not normal to be affected in these ways. One example is people. When I would cross the path of a complete stranger, in that awkward moment, I would look into their eyes.

Whenever I did, something would instantly bother me about them. Or, on the flipside, I would feel a close connection to them.

At first glance, I either feel drawn to them, or I want to deck them square in the nose. I would never really, of course. That's just how I always felt. I know there will always be someone who doesn't like you. However, I really felt it was more than just a normal human nature thing. Something inside told me there had to be more. It was not until much later, I found out why this was.

It was one Tuesday morning when all of this became evident. It was when this world of mine, which I've created, came crashing down, and changed my outlook on my existence.

The moment I awoke that foggy morning, I knew it was going to be very different.

My alarm clock went off, and I hit the snooze button, only to hear the alarm go off again a few seconds later, it seemed. When the alarm sounded a second time, it did not sound like it should have. I heard the voice of a creepy old man, mimicking the sound of the alarm.

I opened my eyes and sat up, and saw nothing. I know I heard a voice, but there was no one there.

A tingling sensation covered my body as that disturbing sound of the man's voice replayed in my ears. I tried to ignore it, and I lay back down, staring at the spinning ceiling fan above. I was so damn tired from the many sleepless nights. I didn't want to deal with all that had been happening to me anymore. I just had to rest more, just a little longer. I closed my eyes.

# 2
# SPECIAL DELIVERY

EEP! BEEP! BEEP! "Caleb!" Tiana said, nudging me. "Turn off the alarm, and get up. You keep hitting the snooze. You're going to be late again."

"Er…uh…okay. I'm good. I won't be late. I'm up," I mumbled. I reached over and turned off the alarm clock, and damn, was I sleepy.

"Don't forget to mail those letters on the way, please," she added.

"Yes, Tiana, I know. I won't forget."

I went to check on little Taylor in her room and saw she was sleeping peacefully and kissed her forehead. I really wanted to go back to bed. There was no way I would. As my grandfather used to always tell me, "If you wanna keep your shit, work for your shit."

Always keeping my girls fed and taking care of is my job—this is what motivates me. I grabbed my clothes and shoes and headed towards the restroom. "Love you, honey, I'll text you later," I said.

Tiana replied, "Love you, too."

*Did I really hear that creepy voice?* Knowing it was just the alarm clock, I shook it off and splashed water on my face. There I stood, looking at myself in the mirror, and noticed something seemed off. I leaned in closer, looking at my reflection. *The eyes were squinting?*

I gazed closer into the reflected eyes that was before me, waiting for it to happen again. Nothing happened. I wasn't sure what I saw. Clearly, I was just tired. I turned to walk out of the bathroom and instantly felt a disturbing presence. I stopped and slowly turned around as if the mirror was drawing me back to it. When I looked back, it was as If I was looking at another person.

"What the?" I muttered in disbelief. The hairs on my neck stood up. *I'm sleepwalking again!* I splashed more water on my face, rubbing my eyes to wake up. I leaned in close, and when I did there was no mistaking it. The movements in the mirror were off. This face I'm seeing before me was not mine. It started making movements and gestures at me. Unable to look away, I continued staring at the bizarre reflection before me.

The face portrayed a serious, intense stare as my heart started beating fast. A disturbing, evil smirk appeared. Frightened, I jumped back as I heard, "Remember, nothing can beat a smile! Ah ha-ha-ha!" The reflection in the mirror had said this, and followed it with eerie, sarcastic laughter. "No!" I yelled. I backpedaled to get out of there, and slipped on the bathroom floor.

"No!" I again yelled with my head down and hands outstretched towards the entity in the mirror. I jumped back to my feet and ran out of the bathroom, slamming the door behind me.

*What the hell? This can't be real!* I thought, confused and in shock.

My first thoughts were to tell Tiana, which I didn't after what she'd already been through. It's just me. I rushed downstairs and grabbed my bag and keys.

Tiana yelled from upstairs, "Post office and the trash!"

"Okay, honey, I will. Love you."

I grabbed the letter and trash, and headed out the door.

It's hard to go to the post office, or to see a letter or stamp. To pass a mail truck or mailman, will always tear me up. However, I know my dad would want me to be strong. I arrived at the post office and noticed the long line. While I was in line, only one person could be heard; a heavyset woman in a raggedy red dress, yapping away. She was a few people ahead of me, and talked nonstop.

People like this you try to subconsciously block out and ignore. But this lady, damn!

On and on she jabbered as her head bobbed and nodded. Her arms and hands were waving and pointing. I really felt for the person she was talking to.

I looked at the time 9:14 a.m., and knew I was going to be late, which didn't bother me. However, this lady did. No way in hell would I be able to endure Miss Chatterbox much longer. Even worse, I saw there was only one person behind the counter.

*This is ridiculous!* I thought.

And then something caught my attention.

*Did I just hear my name?* I wondered. I looked over and realized the odd Asian lady in the red dress had said it. I focused on what she was saying, and in between the meaningless gibberish I was completely floored. I distinctly heard through her ramblings, "Caleb, are you listening? Gah! I didn't hit him. Turn the fan off. Caleb? Ireland!"

Could it be, through the meaningless gibberish, she was talking to me? *No way. Clearly, it's another Caleb,* I thought.

Curious, I looked over at her again and saw she had her back to me. I stepped out of the line for a closer look at what this other Caleb looked like.

There was no other person there. She'd been talking to herself the whole time! The person ahead of her had his back to her, and the people all around her had been ignoring her.

*This woman is completely nuts!*

She stopped talking and casually walked out of the line to the exit. I was almost certain I didn't know this woman, but I wanted a closer look. As she walked toward me, her head was low. She focused her gaze on the ground. I could see she was whispering something I couldn't make out.

As she passed me, I got an uneasy feeling. This time there was no mistaking who she was talking to. The mysterious lady walked over to me, leaned into me, and said in a low grumble, "Oh, your cries have been heard all along, Caleb...."

The hair on my neck stood up. I replied, "I'm sorry, ma'am, do I know you?"

There was no response as she continued walking, never looking back. "Excuse me? Hey!" I said more loudly, as the woman walked out the exit door. I followed her outside as she headed up the sidewalk.

"Hey! Excuse me! Ma'am! What was that you said to me?" I shouted, through the chatter of the other passersby.

Again, no response from her. I ran faster, to catch up, as she turned the corner. When I turned the corner right behind her, to my surprise, she was gone.

*No way did that just happen*, I thought, confused as hell. *What's going on here?*

Through the crowds of people, all around and down both ends of the street, I looked for her. She was nowhere to be found. It was as if she had vanished into thin air.

*My cries have been heard? What the hell does that mean?* I wondered. I headed back to the post office, scratching my head in utter disbelief.

I walked back inside and noticed the line still hadn't moved much, and recognized the same people who had been next to her.

I asked if they remembered seeing the odd woman, and to my surprise, they had no clue who I was referring to.

*How could anyone miss her, when she'd been right there, talking her ass off the whole time not even ten minutes ago? Clearly, I really am losing it.*

Unable to comprehend what just happened, I let it go. I mailed off the letter, and I headed to work.

# 3

# DONUTS, ANYONE?

ON THE WAY to work, I called Tiana and told her what had just happened. She dismissed it all as circumstantial, and said I was sleep-deprived. *Whatever it is, I was freaked out.* I turned the radio on, to help me get my mind off of it.

Running a little behind, I stopped to grab a few dozen donuts.

I arrived at work feeling as good as ever, in spite of a very odd morning. I wasn't going to let some whack-job ruin my day. I walked inside and was quickly greeted with, "Well, good morning, Mr. McCray, we flipping today?" It was Moe, the security guy. For many years, even on mornings like this, old man Moe Frank had always found a way to make me crack a grin and laugh.

"Morning, Moe! Oh yes, you know we're flipping!" I replied.

Moe and I had this thing we started a while back, when one day a penny fell out of my pocket and I looked down at the penny and left it.

Moe picked the penny up and tried to give it back to me. "Ha!

No thanks. How the hell did I have a penny, anyway? I'm allergic to them. You keep it." I said.

Moe replied, "You kidding me? Damn right I'll keep it! Anything that comes from you is bound to bring me luck!"

I laughed and replied, "No. Actually, I do want it back, then," jokingly.

Moe laughed and said, "All right, I tell you what, let's flip for it. If I win, I will own it. If you win then it's yours. Whoever does win, however, will not only own it, but they will also own the day as well."

So ever since that day we have been alternating flips with that same penny to see who will own the day.

Oddly enough, it's been scarily accurate, with the loser always seeming to have a day to forget. Not that I wished anything bad on him. I just loved it when I won and saw his day come to shit. Somehow, I would mostly win, and when I did it was multiple wins in a row. I'd won five days straight, and of course old Moe was not happy about it. Moe called it, I flipped, and I won again. I couldn't help but laugh as he cussed up a storm calling me lucky. Moe would always call tails, for some reason—out of stubbornness, I thought.

I asked Moe, one day, "Why always tails?"

"It represents the tail-ass end, just as my job," he said. He added that I was always heads since I was the Grande Jefe, or big boss.

Old Moe—there's a good man.

Like my father, I was also good at my line of work. I knew I could never outdo my Dad, but I always tried to mirror him. I was the top performer here at Wayland Financial Inc., and had been for a while. I came in killing it and had been consistent, with solid results, like clockwork. And the higher-ups? Yeah, they loved their bonuses, courtesy of me, and being late on this particular morning was the least of my worries. I could do no wrong.

Tiana always told me not to let any of it go to my head, as overconfidence always leads to a big fall. Bullshit, I say to that. From all the everyday praises and recognition and ass-kissing, to my many awards and bonuses—damn, it felt so good, and it had me wanting more. Word had it I was up for promotion, straight to senior finance director. I was so ready for it.

I rushed over to the conference room for a last-minute meeting, and on my way, I ran into Jim Barnes. There's always got to be the jealous asshole looking for every chance to knock you down. And Jim was that guy. He'd been waiting for every opportunity to catch me slipping. Being at the top, I knew I had to always watch my back.

Old Jim had a criminal record for attempted robbery at a We-Cash, check cashing store many years before. He was always looking for quick buck or for any edge over other people. How could anyone employ him, you ask? Well it's easy. Know-it-all Jimbo had dirt on one of the corporate seniors, and Jim made sure they knew of it, with a little blackmail.

"McCray, good morning. Oh, donuts. Thanks, man," he said sarcastically. Funny guy, this guy.

He thought I had no clue what he had been saying and trying to do for a year, as he tried to degrade my character and take my position. He knew I was late, and I knew he would bring it up at some point.

"Morning, Jim," I replied walking past him into the conference room as the meeting was getting underway. The atmosphere seemed tense. All eyes were on me. "Pardon me, everyone, I'll be right back" the speaker said as he walked out of the room. I headed over to the concession table, where I put the donuts, and quietly greeted those around me. "Donuts, anyone?" I asked.

*Damn it!* I thought. Of all people, my boss, Mr. Jacobson, was there, which meant the meeting was important.

"Good morning, Caleb," Mr. Jacobson said. My heart went

ninety to nothing as he leaned in close and whispered, "Well done. I'm very happy and appreciate you."

I was confused. Mr. Jacobson turned and faced everyone else, and said, "Today is a benchmark." He turned back to me and shook my hand with a smile. "Congratulations, Caleb McCray," he said, and everyone cheered.

While I was shaking his hand all I could think about was how confused I was. "For nineteen years, now, we have had a record that no one came close to matching. And today I'm delighted to finally say that the record for the highest annual numbers and accuracy percentage has been broken." Cheers and applause erupted around me, and I stood there in total shock.

They said I had a chance to catch the record, midway through the third quarter, until I hit a ditch. In fact, I didn't even bother keeping track anymore. "This individual, for four years, has done nothing but grow stronger and has become a great asset to this company. Furthermore, I want to double-congratulate our newest senior director of originations, Mr. Caleb McCray!" Tingles surged through my body. In a daze, I stood there as Mr. Jacobson shook my hand.

I felt as If I could levitate as the cheers grew louder. "Congrats, Caleb!" said Shelly, my coworker, as she slid her hand across my back with a wink. Goodness, I had tried hard to stay away from her, as I knew she would be trouble for me. Shit, though, it's the little things she does.

I gave my appreciation speech, thanked everyone, and we headed to Tom's Pub to celebrate after work.

# 4

# A TOAST

O N THE WAY to Tom's I called Tiana to check on her and asked if she wanted to go. She hadn't been feeling well lately and I knew she would decline, which she did. I told her to lock up and sleep well. I would see her in the morning. I pulled into Tom's parking lot and did a quick mirror check. *Yup, still a Don.* Again, I thought of that crazy woman from the post office. What she said really got to me.

*Your cries have been heard? It has to mean something. This is unreal!* I thought.

I walked inside, and I greeted everyone and made my way to the table. Jason came over, handed me a cold one.

"A toast…" Jay started to say, and Shelly walked over to my other side. She leaned into me and said, "Congrats, handsome. Is your wife coming?" She put her arm around my waist. "Shelly! I didn't know you were coming. No, she's not; she's a little under the weather." She grinned and massaged my side.

Jay continued, with his beer raised high, saying, "A toast to a great guy, a great family man, and my best friend. And to the best Wayland employee...Caleb McCray!" I smiled at Jay, thanking him, and raised my mug to Shelly's as we toasted. She smelt so damn good! Her sexy look and beautiful eyes pierced straight to my soul as a warm feeling overtook me.

From that moment, I never took my eyes off Shelly.

I glanced around the room as the others continued to cheer and clap. Another person shouted, "Shots!" Another round of shots, and another we took.

The room started spinning around me. I tried to focus on what Jay was saying and couldn't.

"We going to BL's, Caleb?" Jay asked me. BL's is BabeLand's, one of the most prestigious gentlemen's clubs we go to.

In spite of knowing I was already past my limit, I pointed at Jay with a raised brow, raising my beer, saying, "Does a hooker accept cash?"

"Shit yeah, we're going!" I replied.

Shelly rode with me as we pulled up and parked at BL's. She moved over closer, caressed my neck, and rubbed my inner thighs. She leaned in and kissed me. "Damn it!" I said. "Shelly, you're driving me insane!" I kissed her again and we headed inside.

Walking into BL's, I was greeted by the valets and doorman. Half-naked dancers of unbelievable beauty were all over, giving me alluring stares. "Hello, Mr. McCray, want your same spot?" Marty the manager asked.

"For sure, Marty, thanks," I replied. We headed straight to the VIP section, where champagne, beer, and shots covered the table, with dancers already there, waiting.

"Shots!" Shelly shouted, while another dancer straddled my lap and began to grind on me. Shelly caressed my head and neck while kissing another female dancer. All I could hear was the thumping of the loud music and laughter. Thick smoke filled the room.

I heard an announcement: "All right, all right, ladies and gents. Give it up for Karissma, to the main stage! Holy shit. Is she sexy as hell, or what? Give it up for her, fellas. Also, we got half-priced shots and $3.50 you-call-it's going on for the next hour. So c'mon, fellas, let's make it happen!" It was the DJ, over the loudspeaker.

I looked around and saw some guy saying something to me. I couldn't make it out. Shelly was kissing and rubbing all over me. The music got louder as another girl put her bare breasts in my face.

I knocked my full beer over, and watched it spill to the ground. I was losing it. The smell of another tequila shot made me gag as I turned my head, trying to hide it. I closed my eyes, blocking it all for a second. Out of nowhere I heard, "Hey, baby? You okay?"

I rubbed my eyes and opened them.

It was Shelly! I was in bed with Shelly? No!

"What time is it?" I asked.

"It's almost one p.m. You should sleep."

"Where are we?" I asked.

I sat up and saw I was totally naked and covered up, looking for my clothes. "We're at my house, honey. Are you hungry?"

*Her house? What the fuck?*

I tried to recall the night before, but it was all a blur.

"You okay?" Shelly asked as I put my shirt and pants on.

"Yeah. Just a bathroom and aspirin and I'll be good," I replied.

"Of course. Down the hall, to the right" Shelly said. I headed to the bathroom and felt my cellphone vibrate in my pocket. I had five missed calls and a lot of texts from Tiana.

I looked over the texts from her from the night before. Dammit! And all my broken, drunken texts. I'm going to crash at Jason's, *I texted her?*

Without another word to Shelly, I got my things and rushed

out the door and headed home. On the way I noticed a text from Tiana, saying, "Whenever you decide to come home, DO NOT talk to me!"

I called Tiana, but there was no answer.

I was completely disgusted with myself when I pulled into my driveway. I walked in as Nalla jumped on me with her sloppy kisses. "Daddy!" my little girl, Taylor, shouted with excitement, jumping up in my arms.

"Oh, it's my big girl! Daddy missed you so much!" I replied as I kiss her head and cheek.

I told Taylor to head back to the living room to watch cartoons as I tried to muster the strength to walk up and face Tiana.

*Oh, shit!* I smelled Shelly's perfume on my shirt.

I see Tiana in the bathroom and sneak into my closet to change shirts. After some of her yelling and a few curse-words, we talked and I was somehow able to smooth things over. All it took was a night out.

Later that night I tucked in Little Taylor and joined Tiana in bed. My mind began to race. I was tired of thinking about it all. I turned on my side, ready to pass out.

# 5

# INTO THE NIGHT

*S*CREECH! "HUH?" *WHAT was that?* I heard something by the window, an odd sound coming from outside. *Screech!* The noise got louder, sounding like something scratching the side of the house. With Tiana and Taylor fast asleep, I got up and walked over to the window. I saw nothing. *It's just some animal, I'm sure.*

A strong urge took over. I had to go check it out, as if I were drawn to something outside. I got out of bed and walked out through the dim lighting of my living room, and peeked through the blinds. Again, I saw nothing. I unlocked the front door and walked into the cold onto the porch.

The sounds of the night echo in my ears. I heard crickets, howls, and dog barks. I didn't even think twice I was shirtless with only my boxers on as I cautiously walked down the rickety steps to the front yard. I was a little concerned, being totally defenseless, without my pistol. I continued looking for the mysterious noise.

I heard an eerie owl's hoot in the distance just as a black cat ran in front of me. There I stood, completely still, as a sharp chill shot up my spine. "Shit!" I yelled out when I stepped on a rock.

A feeling of being watched hit me.

My instinct said to get the hell back in the house. My legs and feet, however, didn't budge, thinking of Taylor and Tiana. I put my fears aside and looked all around. There was nothing.

I walked through the backyard and saw it was okay, and headed back to the front. *Clang!* Down the street I heard what sounded like someone took a bat to a car in the street. I walked to the middle of the street for a better look. Again, a strong feeling of being watched overcame me as I frantically looked around. *What is that?* I heard a deep growl to my right. I turned and focused down the street, toward the noise, and got a tingly sensation all over. There through the darkness I saw something.

In the distance, standing in the middle of the street, I noticed a dark, shadowy figure. My heart started to pound and my nose started to run. I wiped my nose and realized it was blood. Nose bleeds had always plagued my fears. The hairs on the back of my neck stood up. In spite of initially wanting to run, I let my curiosity get the best of me and wanted a closer look. I wanted to know who or what was before me.

I took a few steps toward the figure and noticed the figure was also walking toward me. I stopped and the dark figure in the distance continued to move toward me. *This has to be another damn dream,* I thought while rubbing my eyes. Blood continued pouring from my nose onto my chest and the ground. *This thing is heading right to me!* I took a few steps back, to draw whatever it was away from my house. Closer the dark figure got, and I turned and started running.

Down the middle of the street I dashed as fast I could. "Oh, shit!" I said, glancing back to see the figure chasing me. Faster and faster I continued to run into the brisk of the night. Through neighbor's yards and in between parked cars, I ran hoping to throw them off. I turned behind the corner of a house. There I knelt and caught my breath. I carefully peeked around the side of the house, and to my surprise they were gone.

Suddenly it hit me "Tiana! Taylor!" They were alone and the house was vulnerable. I ran back to the house and saw my front door was shut. I ran through the door and up the stairs to the room, to find they were still fast asleep and okay. *Did this really just happen? Someone has got to be messing with me here.* Delirious and exhausted, I knew I needed rest.

# 6
# THINGS TO COME

THAT NEXT MORNING and the following week, in fact, were pretty much more of the same routine. Go to work, secretly see Shelly, and more late-night drinking. All while balancing the home life. Tiana began to question my many late nights at the office. I continued to deny and cover it all up, to make it right.

All was well again. What still bothered me were all of the bizarre ordeals that had been happening to me. However, I was not going to let that stop me from living.

Keeping busy and keeping my mind focused on other things were key. One way of doing this was with another pastime of mine: poker. I'd been crushing the guys over at Lucky B's, a private club. The place is loaded with a bunch of donkeys, who gave me their money regularly. Lucky's is the hottest underground poker gig in town, which I play a few times a month. It's owned by another shady guy named Big Larry Saunders.

No-limit hold 'em poker cash game is my game, and when

you win big around here people notice. And when you win a lot, people start to talk about it and monitor you closely.

I was up on these guys roughly $34,000, the last three sessions. Now the yahoos at Lucky's were getting their panties in a wad, because of my lack of action as of late. It started at my last poker session, where I heard smartass comments, which I brushed off. When one guy hinted that I went gray, cheating or ratting and shit—that was when it got personal.

I may be a lot of things, but I'm no cheater. I don't have to cheat. Pretty funny guys, who cry when they lose. I purposely kept my winnings away for a while, so they would sulk.

Eventually, back at home, Tiana started acting very different, and by then I knew she suspected something.

I do love Tiana with all my heart, and I'm not even sure what the hell I was doing with Shelly and with things. I had no answers. It's a need, and the attention that always needs to be satisfied with me. All I knew, I could never leave Tiana or my little girl.

That week, things started to change. It was on this particular Friday night that everything started to go in another direction.

Early in the day, I asked if she wanted to join me for drinks at Tom's Pub after work. Normally, she would be all over it. And she said yes; however, it was like she didn't really want to. I could tell something was wrong with how she'd been acting.

With Tiana suspecting me of cheating, and Shelly now acting weird, along with the other odd things going on, I was getting worn down. On the way to Tom's I got a text from JC Stokes, my bookie. He's high on his Mexican heritage. His text read, "Hey, man. Sorry to tell you, Duke didn't cover and you lost the Auburn game. Just wanting to update where we're at now. Total for this week is -$4,330.00 and grand total for the month is $-18,950.00. Adding that to what you owe prior is $-56,350.00. Your balance is way over and I'm going to need that quick. I cannot wait on it like last time. Need this settled now. Let me know ASAP. Thanks."

*Am I really reading this text right now? Both those damn bets were near guaranteed! I lost last week and now I take two huge hits this week?*

After work, I headed to the parking garage, and ran into old man Moe, the head security guard. *Why is he still here?* I wondered. Seeing Moe again reminded me of why the day had been like that. After a long winning streak with our morning coin toss, I finally lost this morning.

"You still here, Moe? Overtime?" I asked. He usually leaves at four p.m. or so, and it was almost six.

He replied, "Yeah, they called me in because some crazy woman was up here a bit ago raising Cain about absolutely nothing. She kept rambling some gibberish talk that made no sense at all. She kept trying to get in."

It had to be the weird lady from the post office. I asked Moe, "Crazy woman, you say? Did they say what she looked like? Could they make out anything she was saying?"

Moe replied, "She was Asian and heavyset, with an orange, torn dress. She kept talking about food and other nonsense. They couldn't really make it all out. They thought she mentioned your name. Funny, huh? Just another wacko. She's gone. All is well."

*Mentioned my name?* I thought. *It was her!* I felt chills.

I nearly pissed myself hearing all of this. I have to get the hell out of there.

"Yeah, that is strange. Well, all right, night."

I headed to the parking garage. I get in my car and immediately texted Shelly. Actually, Espie. That's her codename for my coworker, Shelly Phuentes in my cell phone. Her first name and last name initials pronounced together make Espie.

Tonight, is the perfect night to meet her. I have to get my mind off all of this. I cleared it with Tiana, texting her that I was going to help Jason with a project at his house and would be home later. She replied, "Yup"—that single word she texts when she's mad.

# 7

# NIGHTCAP

THIRTY MINUTES WENT by without a response from Shelly. I got to Tom's and saw the place was dead. Five beers later and still no word or sign of Shelly.

I texted her, "Hey what's up? You okay?"

Shelly responded, "Sorry I'm tired tonight and just went home."

*She went home? Bullshit! Never has she done this before.*

Change of plans. "Ready for another one, Caleb?"

It was Jeff the bartender, a good buddy of mine. I looked and saw it was 6:40 p.m. *Am I really going to be all alone on a Friday night? I can either chalk it up and end this day from hell, or say screw it and drink it all away here. Yeah, screw it.* "Yes, sir, Mr. Harmen. In fact, I'll need a chaser for my beer. I'll take two shots of Don Julio."

Jeff laughed and said, "You got it, man!" The hour went by, and after a lot of small talk and a few more drinks I was feeling good.

*I really miss Tiana and my little girl. What am I even doing here?* I wondered. "You can close me out when ready, Jeff," I said. I'm going to go home and make it right. I'm going to take my family out tonight.

I downed my last beer, closed out my tab, and headed out. *I don't need Shelly; I don't need my work; I don't need anyone. I just want my family!*

"See you around, Jeff," I said, as I headed toward the exit.

"You're okay to drive home, right, Caleb?"

*What the hell did this guy just ask me? As if he doesn't know me or something.*

"C'mon, man, you know me. Of course, I'm good!"

"Okay, I know, just making sure. You seem a little on the tipsy side. More than usual".

I gave Jeff a wink and headed out the door.

I got in my car and sent one last text to Shelly: "Hey cool thanks. Cuz yeah, I'm sick too. *cough cough*"

I called Tiana, telling her I was on the way and to get dressed because we were going out. She was shocked and said okay.

Maybe she really believed I was with Jay. If anything, taking her and Taylor out always patches things up. She loved being together as a family.

I sprayed a little cologne on, popped in a breath mint, and walked into the house. There was my baby girl, watching her cartoons. She said, "Daddy!" and ran into my arms.

"Daddy missed you so much. Are you hungry? Let's go eat," I said as my little Taylor looked up at me with a big smile.

"Hey, honey" Tiana said from the kitchen.

"Babe!" I replied, giving her a kiss and hug and head out.

We headed to Tiana's favorite place: Oshana's sushi restaurant. "Caleb, have you been drinking? You're slurring" Tiana said.

"I had a few beers at Jay's before I came. I'm okay, honey," I replied.

*I better take things slow. I do feel tipsy.*

The night sky was clear with bright stars. Taylor smiled happily. A perfect night to go out, and I was glad I'd made this choice. I glanced over at Tiana and, damn it, she was looking hot. "Caleb! You're almost going eighty, slow down! The speed limit is seventy."

"I'm sorry, baby girl. I'm sorry. I'm slowing down."

We got to Oshana's and enjoyed each other, and for once I felt stress-free. A few sakes and a nice meal together made a great night with my family. A feeling I had not felt in a long time. "Thank you, Daddy, for being with us for dinner," my little girl said, smiling, and leaned her head on my arm.

"You're welcome, my pretty girl," I replied.

"Yes, thank you for dinner, honey," Tiana said. "I guess no more word from your girlfriend?"

My jaw dropped. I couldn't believe what I'd heard. "My Girlfriend?" I hesitantly replied.

"Yeah, you know the one, from the post office?" Tiana replied.

"Ha! Nope. Nothing," I replied.

"Was there anything else? Did you guys save room for dessert?" the waitress asked.

"Yay, dessert!" Little Taylor shouted with excitement. Tiana laughed.

"Very well, the little princess has spoken, so dessert it is!" I said. "I know my wife said earlier that this looked good, so that's what we'll have."

At this point you would think I wouldn't even think of Shelly, but I did. I mustered a distraction and pointed to the dessert picture and handed the menu to Tiana. "Right, honey? That's what you wanted?" I asked while sneaking a peek at my cellphone. Still nothing from Shelly. I texted Shelly, telling her I was coming over later.

I put my phone in my front shirt pocket as Tiana said, "Yes that looks good doesn't it?"

I replied, "Yes, perfect! We will take that and another sake, and then close us out."

"Another one?" Tiana said.

"Yes, and then we're out of here," I replied.

We finished and headed to the car. Taylor jumped into my arms on the way out, hugging me tight. "I love you, Daddy," she said, smiling.

"Daddy loves you so much," I replied.

Out of nowhere, my Taylor followed up with a question I didn't expect: "Daddy, when we die, what happens to us? Where do we go?"

I couldn't believe my little girl just asked that, and I didn't know how to answer it. I pondered for a moment how I should answer.

"Well, honey, that's a good question," I said. "We don't really die. When it's time for us to go, we go all the way up on a big cloud. All the way up to heaven." I knew there was no heaven, but that was something she would have to find out later in life, on her own. She could have something to look forward to, at least for now. I didn't know what else to say.

My little girl's eyes lit up, and she smiled ear to ear. "Really? Oh, thank you, Daddy!" Taylor kissed me on the cheek, and hugged my neck.

Tiana said, "That's right, honey; we all fly up, and go to heaven."

I leaned in the back of the car to put Taylor in her car seat and lost my balance. I nearly fell with Taylor in my arms.

"Caleb, really?" Tiana yelled.

"I'm fine, honey. There's a damn stump sticking out of the asphalt over here that I tripped on."

I leaned down again to put Taylor in the backseat and heard something drop.

"You dropped something, Daddy," Taylor said. "I'll help you." Taylor tried to help.

"No, it's okay, honey. Thank you, though," I replied.

All I wanted was to hurry home, knowing I was getting some tonight, if not with Tiana then with Shelly. I could tell Tiana was feeling frisky.

Finally, I got Taylor in the car seat and we headed home. *Why do I feel like I'm forgetting something all of a sudden?*

*My wallet!* I thought, while feeling my back pocket for my wallet. It was there.

"You want me to drive?" Tiana asked.

"I'll drive. I'm okay," I replied.

I just wanted to get home.

# 8

# ARE WE THERE YET?

O N THE WAY home, it all played in my head, what Moe said that batty lady was saying. I knew it was the same woman from the post office. There had to be more to it "Slow down, Caleb! Its sixty through here, and it's foggy."

"Tiana, I'm fine," I said.

"Momma, are we there yet?" asked Taylor.

"Almost, honey" Tiana replied.

I heard my phone vibrate. "Here, Daddy, someone's calling for you," Taylor said.

*Calling me? Oh shit, she has my phone!*

That's what I was bothered by earlier! It fell out of my damn shirt pocket, putting Taylor in her car seat.

All I knew was I had to get that phone before Tiana. I reached back for my phone, but it was too late. "Here, Taylor" Tiana said with her hand already reached back, taking the phone. *No!* If I tried to take the phone from Tiana, she would wonder why. She would know I was trying to hide something.

"It's Jay, I'm sure, just ignore it," I said as I reached for the phone.

"No, it says missed call from Espie. Who's Espie?" Tiana asked.

"Oh, that's a buddy from work."

"A buddy?"

Normally I would instantly come back with a perfect response and get out of this. Right now, however, I feel woozy. I'm having a hard time thinking clearly.

No matter what I said, I knew it wouldn't work. She was going through my entire phone.

Her face showed utter shock and disgust as she went through all the texts and calls between me and Shelly. All of which I forgot to delete. *I have to stop her; I have to get my phone now!*

I played dumb, saying, "Huh? What are you talking about? Give me the phone," while reaching over to grab it.

"No, Caleb!" Tiana yelled back, pushing my hand away. "Who the hell is Espie? Huh? Tell me! Oh my God!"

I shrugged while shaking my head, "No, it's not like that."

"Don't even try that bullshit with me Caleb! Stop, it's a red light!"

I had to say something. I replied, "I have no clue how they got my number, Tiana. I think Jay at work is messing with me. It's not *like* that. For a second, I even thought it was you and just went along with it."

*What the hell did I just say?* I reached out again for the phone while Tiana leaned away, blocking my hand. "Oh my God…oh my God! Are you fucking kidding me?"

It looked like this was it. This was the night it would all unfold, and the motherfucking jig was up. I knew I couldn't hide this forever, and now this was out I actually feel relieved.

"I knew it! I knew you were cheating on me! I knew it!"

"Tiana! Calm down! Do not yell like that in front of Taylor! Give me my damn phone!"

She pushed my hand away.

"Daddy, Momma, please don't fight!" little Taylor cried out.

"Tiana, see? You're upsetting Taylor!"

I looked back at Taylor, to reassure her. She continued to cry. Her little head was down in her lap with her hands covering her face. I reached back and held her little hand. "Please don't cry, honey. It's okay, baby girl." I said.

Words could not express the anger that consumed me. I looked over at Tiana to see her mouth moving while pointing her finger in my face and hitting the dashboard. I wrestled her for the phone.

"Daddy, please!" Taylor desperately cried out.

"I'm not hurting momma, it's okay," I told her.

I just wanted Taylor not to be upset anymore. *I can't think!*

I saw Taylor hunched over, crying harder, and Tiana devastated, unable to catch her breath.

"You both have been sending pics? You even text her at the restaurant that you're coming over? With me and Taylor with you? How could you? I hate you!"

"Tiana, please, I'm sorry!" I pleaded.

"Caleb…oh my God! Watch out!" Tiana screamed.

I looked up through the dense fog and saw I'd veered off the road, heading right toward a concrete divider. "Shit! Hold on!" I yelled as I yanked the wheel hard left, barely missing the divider.

"A tree!" Tiana shouted as I yanked the wheel to the right.

"Caleb!" Tiana cried out in horror.

All I remembered next was reaching back for little Taylor as the car flipped. Over and over we rolled as my head and body slammed back and forth into the seat, door, and steering wheel.

The car stopped upright on all four wheels. I slowly opened my eyes.

I looked over to see Taylor and Tiana lying in their seats, unresponsive. *Oh, no. What have I done? Taylor, no!* "Taylor? Tiana?" My eyes slowly closed against my will.

# 9

# DAGGERED

"WHY, HELLO THERE, sugar, how ya feeling? You're a pretty lucky fella."

Oh, my head hurts… I reached up to my head and felt bandages.

"Try not to touch your head. You got banged up pretty good but you're going to be just fine. Just take it easy and rest, now." I opened my eyes and saw I was in a hospital bed.

"Tiana?" I said. "Where's my daughter? My wife?"

I tried to get out of the bed, but the nurse stopped me.

"Oh, no! Lay back down."

"Are they all right? Is my little girl okay?"

"Yes, they're fine. Don't worry, darling. Your wife and daughter are here and they're okay. Your wife stepped out for a second. She'll be back. You just need to rest, now."

Oh, my ribs! My entire body hurt. Too sore to move, I slowly lay back down.

"I'm Queenie Williamson, your nurse. You can call me nurse

Que." Que covered me back up and said, "You all had quite a scare, I heard. I'm just glad you all are all right."

Tiana walked in with the doctor.

"Hello, Caleb, I'm Dr. Miller. How's your head and ribs feel?" he asked.

"I'm a little sore, but I'm okay, Doctor."

"Caleb, you all are very lucky."

I looked back at Tiana and saw her chin start to quiver.

"You, your wife and daughter were involved in an unfortunate car accident that caused your vehicle to flip over many times when you tried to avoid a passing deer. The good news is, all three of you are going to be okay. Your wife sustained minor injuries and you got a few minor lacerations and some bruised ribs."

Dr. Miller continued, "Little Taylor, I regret to say, was not as fortunate. She flew out of her car seat, as it appeared her straps either failed or weren't fastened properly. She was thrown around pretty good. As a result, and in spite of emergency surgery and our best efforts, she lost the use of her left arm. Although she is responsive, she is unable to speak at this time. We cannot explain it. We are continuing to run tests and do all we can with therapy and treatment. She will be here for a bit. I'm deeply sorry."

I sat, completely motionless, as the room spun around me. My heart was daggered. *Oh God, what have I done? What did I do to my little girl? I didn't buckle her in right. I made us crash. How did they not detect my alcohol level? It's all my fault! It's all because of me this happened! I will never forgive myself for this! I hate my fucking self!* I thought.

Unable to hold back all the pain and anger, I looked at Tiana and cried.

Twelve days later, I continued to ignore all texts and calls from work and anyone else, and I didn't care. Knowing the last few months had been tight financially would have to be put on hold. I would deal with it once Taylor was okay.

The memory of that night plagued me. I would never be the same. *How could I?*

"Well, okay. Dr. Miller said little Taylor is doing a lot better and can go home. Just know that God's in control and my prayers are with you all," said nurse Que.

*God's in control of this? God's with us and she's going to pray?* Hearing what Que just said was the last thing I wanted to hear.

"He's in control, huh?" I said. "Thanks."

We headed to the car and loaded up.

"Now you all take good care of this little precious angel. When you leave this place don't look back!" Nurse Que said behind us. I turned around to thank her, and when I did, she was gone.

*What the heck?* I thought. *Either she disappeared, or is a hell of fast runner.*

We got in the car and headed home.

# 10

## HELLO AGAIN

A T HOME, THAT night, I tried talking with Tiana again. It didn't go well. Bearing the guilt and shame of what I did had started to hit me harder.

We all needed a good night's rest.

It didn't take long for them to fall asleep. I, on the other hand, could not.

It was another restless night, tossing and turning, staring at my ceiling fan, trying to shake off what I did to my little girl. My mind wouldn't turn off. A familiar uneasy feeling took over as I was reminded of all the sleepless nights I'd had before. I turned the TV on to help me sleep, and I feel my eyelids grow heavy.

<Shelly! No…Uh. Crazy lady—what's it mean? Ah. The poker game, bet the hand…no, please. Our bills; need money…Tiana… Uh…Daddy, where do we go when we die? We have heard you, Caleb…Car seat…Oh, uh, eighty-three mph. No! A wall. Crash!>

"Taylor!" I shouted, sitting up. Breathing heavily, I looked over at Tiana and Taylor and saw they were sleeping peacefully. I'm okay. *These dreams seem so damn real!*

I lay down again and closed my eyes to the sound of the ceiling fan.

"Caleb!" Out of nowhere I heard a man's raspy voice call my name. I sat up, looking

around the dark room, and saw nothing. Something didn't feel right. An eerie feeling overtook

me again. A few moments later, I heard soft whispering outside my window. The hairs on the back of my neck stood up.

I walked over and looked out the window, and I saw nothing out of the ordinary. I looked up and noticed the moon was extremely bright. It was as if the gleaming moon was calling to me.

Again, I let my curiosity get the best of me, headed down to the living room, and peeked through the blinds. When I did, I saw something. Through the darkness of the night I noticed a figure standing out in the middle of the street, looking right at me. Chills shot up my spine and slowly I moved away from the window.

*What the shit?* I said to myself.

My initial thought was to call the police, and for some reason I didn't. I went to my closet and grabbed my baseball bat. In a surge of anger, I opened the front door and yelled, "What the fuck do you want?"

There was no one there.

I wanted to make sure whoever was there was gone, as I grabbed my keys and locked the front door. I walked outside and tossed the keys in a nearby bush.

I was shirtless in my boxers. The cold of the night hit my body as I walked through the front yard gripping my bat tightly, ready for anything. I proceeded to the middle of the street, where they were standing.

A loud bird cackled from above. I looked up as a black crow

with glowing white eyes stood on the streetlight, looking down at me.

"Ka-caw! Ka-caw!" the crow screamed, as if trying to commu-nicate with me. I felt a presence behind me. A deep fear overtook me as blood splats hit the asphalt from my nose.

I knew I was being watched.

I slowly turned around and there the dark shadowy figure stood in the street. Completely frozen, I was unable to move, as I continued staring at this bizarre figure before me. Like a déjà-vu from hell, it all seemed too familiar. It was from the other night.

Frightened, I raised my bat and clinched it tighter as I started to backpedal. "Who are you?" I yelled to the stranger of the night who didn't respond. Nothing but the sounds of crickets and howls of the animals of night. Paranoid, I looked again at my house, and all around me, thinking there may be more than one of them.

I looked back at the figure again, and when I did the figure ran right toward me. "Oh shit!" I said as I turned and ran.

I dropped my bat. It hit my knee, and I tripped on the curb. I couldn't bring myself to look back, knowing they were almost on top of me. I saw the bat next to me, reached for it, and heard, "Ka-caw!" The crow swooped down and clutched the bat in its talons, and flew away. I hear the trampling of steps behind me, closer and closer, and I got up and I ran to my house.

Through my front yard I dashed up to my porch and forgot which bush I threw the keys into as I sifted through them all. "There it is!" I said and grabbed the keys. My heart beat through my chest as I struggled to get the key in the door. The loud foot-steps behind me drew nearer. I finally opened the door and locked it behind me.

*Wham! Wham!* I heard as the figure slammed into the front door. I saw the knob turn. I grabbed my gun from the cabinet door and reinforced the door all I could.

And just like that it was quiet.

I looked out the front windows, and there was nothing there. Once again, it was like they simply vanished. I secured the rest of the house and regained myself. Trying to come to terms with all of this was just too much.

*It's confirmed, I have truly lost my mind.* Exhausted, I headed back upstairs. *I don't have time for this shit! My family is my only focus. Tomorrow, I'm making this all right.*

# 11

## SAY IT AIN'T SO

T HAT NEXT MORNING, while I was in bed, I tried coming to terms with what had happened. Just who or what was that, chasing me last night? *Why am I halluci-nating all the time?*

I wanted it all behind me. To my surprise, Tiana called me downstairs for the trash I forgot, I'm sure. "Go upstairs and play in your room, honey. Mommy will be up there in a little bit," she told Taylor. I knew we had to get back on track and talk at some point. This is a good opportunity to do it.

I needed to seize this moment and jump right on in. "Honey, listen, I know I have made the worst decision in my life, for what I let happen to Taylor and to you. Words cannot express how I feel right now..." Before I could get another word out, Tiana chimed in, "Caleb, do you love her?"

"No way!" I said. "I was drunk one night and got caught up. She means nothing to me! I already cut her off."

Tiana looked in my eyes for what seemed like an eternity,

while shaking her head in disgust. I noticed a single tear roll down her cheek. She closed her eyes and turned away from me.

I knew she didn't believe me. I knew there was nothing more I could have said. "A police officer called, looking for you, last Tuesday, and I got a call from the mortgage company letting us know the last two payments did not go through. I called and now I know were behind on our car payments. Caleb, are you kidding me? Are you in trouble? What did you do?"

"No, Tiana. I'm not. We're fine. I promise!"

"Caleb! We're losing everything! Oh, God!"

"What are you talking about? That can't be! It's obviously an issue with the bank, and I will call and fix it all tomorrow. Tiana, please don't worry! I will call them first thing in the morning; I will take care of all of that." I reached out my hands to comfort and hold Tiana, and she stepped back. "No!" she yelled, pushing my hands away.

"Bullshit, Caleb! You want to explain to me why a man came looking for you knocking at our house last week?"

*A man? I can't believe this! It's got to be one of JC's henchmen, trying to collect what I owe him,* I thought. *Tiana cannot find out about any of this. Not now! I made a deposit to cover all of this in time. How is any of this happening?*

"Did he say who he was?" I asked Tiana.

She replied, "He said he was a close friend, and he needed something back that you borrowed. He said he would come back another time and walked away."

*That piece of shit! How dare he hit me up to collect at my house! How could I have let any of this happen? How did I get here?*

"Tiana, I promise we're fine, and this will all be fixed tomorrow."

Tiana yelled, "No, Caleb! I just can't! Caleb, I love you very much, but—"

I felt my heart sink and got lightheaded.

"I just can't do this anymore. I cannot live this way, putting our daughter through this any longer. I have to think what's best for her. She needs a full-time father!"

"No, Tiana. Please," I muttered, staring hopelessly at the ground.

"You are not the same person anymore, and for a long while I have seen this coming. I tried to give us and you the benefit of the doubt, for our daughter. I tried talking to you, hinting to you that we needed help! I prayed, I hoped it would all change! And you did nothing!"

The room started spinning all around me. There I sat in utter shock as I began to cry.

"Caleb, I tried so hard to keep all of this from Taylor, faking a normal life for her. It all finally took a toll on me: the lies, home late or not, coming home at all hours, and our finances. Oh, and let's not forget your girlfriend! And your drinking that almost killed our daughter!"

I looked up at Tiana as tears continued to stream down my face. Choked up and barely able to speak, Tiana said, "You don't want this family life anymore, and you don't want me, or us! Caleb, I want a divorce. Goodbye."

# 12

# HEART OF STONE

I COULDN'T FATHOM what I had heard. I was crushed. In spite of many pleas and cries, I ended up moving out that weekend.

I couldn't tell anyone. I shut down all my social media and everyone at work. When my mother found out, she had called me as I was packing to encourage and comfort me. "It will all work out. Don't worry. Everything happens for a reason, for a time, in order to make it all better." It was what she said next that really gripped me. She said, "Maybe it's time for a change, starting within yourself. Do what you know to do at this exact moment, that will get you on the right path going forward. I'm here for you, son. I love you so much."

That stuck with me. I needed to hear it. The day after, I moved out, and got a call from my bank: "Mr. McCray, we have a serious problem. The deposit you made last week was with counterfeit bills. We need to know where you got those bills. We have initiated an investigation."

I was floored. I knew those assholes at the card room paid my poker winnings out in counterfeit bills. *They fucked me!* I furiously thought.

I played dumb, telling the bank representative I had my assistant make the deposit. I added I would help with the investigation. Knowing my response was just a Band-Aid that would quickly fall off, I wasted no time. Next, the cops would be hunting me down, with a bunch of questions that I didn't have answers to. I immediately headed over to Lucky B's.

I couldn't wait to confront that piece of shit, Larry. When I did, Larry claimed they had no clue. In fact, he said he was going to ask me the same thing. He said a player snuck the dirty funds into their room, and when they tracked it, it came back to me.

Those fuckers stuck me! And there was nothing I could do, other than threaten him, which I did, to give my money back and leave. At this point I was starting to lose it.

Even still, with all of this happening, I made time to see Taylor, as I promised, that same day.

Weeks went by and then months. For the first time in my life I was utterly alone. With bills mounting and nothing going right, desperation started to set in, and my mind began to wander. Without Tiana and Taylor in my life, another day was unbearable. I needed my family back!

I knew that in order to get my family back, to get it all back, I needed one thing. I needed money, and I needed it now. And I further knew there was only one way to do this. I turned to the only person I knew who could make this happen. I needed Jim.

In spite of how I felt about him, and against my better judgment, I knew I had no other choice. With Jim, if there was a dollar to be made, he was in, and he was the only person to help me. The company Christmas party was that Saturday, and it was there I would fill him in. This Saturday, I would put my plan in place to get Tiana and Taylor back.

It was the day before the party and my stomach was already in knots. I tried to think of how to bring this up to Jim, as I knew it was going to give him immediate dirt on me.

I pulled up to the hotel where the party was being held and saw it was in full swing. The night was muggy, with slight drizzle. The atmosphere was festive, with cheers and laughs all around, making it easy to hide in plain sight. There's Jim, standing by the stairs, with Peter his little sidekick shit. I walked over and greeted them, "Hey Barnes. Hey Pete, Merry Christmas."

Thrown off, Jim replied, "Oh damn, well Merry Christmas, McCray," sarcastically.

With a grin, I subtly grabbed Jim's drink and poured it on top of Pete's head, and bitch-slapped Jim in the face.

No. That's not what I did, really. But oh, dammit, did I want to.

I asked Jim, "Can I talk to you a second?"

We headed outside and lit up smokes, and I explained everything. In a matter of minutes, we had dirt on each other. I knew of his criminal history, which was covered up, and now he knew I was asking for bad money. I said, "I know of your tax troubles and I think we both could use a little help pretty quick, am I right?"

Now that I had his attention, I added, "I figured you would have an idea or two for some fast cash. What do you say?"

Jimbo looked into my eyes with a smirk, releasing a puff of smoke, and replied, "How much you need and how soon do you need it?"

I let out a sigh of relief, knowing Jim was in. He told me he'd had a perfect plan for a while that was ready to go, and he needed the right person.

Jimbo proposed an old-fashioned bank heist, and he knew the perfect and easiest place to do it: Westside Bank. He knew someone who used to work there, in the security department. With some negotiation, Jim was able to obtain all of the security details and the building's schematics, and exactly where and when to hit it.

Wow! I couldn't believe my ears! *How perfect is this?* I thought. "It's a guaranteed lick," Jim said with a wink. "I'm going to call you tonight with the rest of the details. Oh, and Caleb." Jim grabbed my arm. "Remember, you came to me. We both have a lot to lose, our lives, our families…don't fuck me, Caleb. It will be your last fuck if you do."

I nodded, and agreed. I couldn't believe I was actually talking about this; however, I was ready. I was in, and there was no backing out. Jim gave me the last few details as we heard a noise from behind us, a thud that came from behind the door.

"Who's there?" Jim asked.

To our surprise, out of the dark corner, Shelly walked out with a subtle grin.

"Shelly?" I said, surprised.

"Pardon me. Surely you boys aren't planning on making a withdrawal without me, are you?"

I nearly passed out. Jim and I knew she heard it all and wanted a piece. We were fucked. We had no choice but to bring her in. With our careers and lives at stake, we all three swore secrecy, and proceeded as planned.

Shelly threw us all off by proposing a backup plan. I always knew she was very odd and a little off, always looking out for what's best for her alone. What she said, though, neither of us were prepared for. She said, "Listen, I know I don't bring much to the table. What I can do is save us all if it goes bad." She continued telling us of some sort of sacred ritual practice she had been experimenting with. A sort of bizarre time warp séance in the supernatural she claimed really worked.

She insisted that it was possible to travel to another time or dimension, and that she had already done it. Knowing Shelly, I didn't doubt it. Beautiful or not, this chick was weird. With looks of serious doubt on our faces, Shelly took out her cell and showed us clips and stories online. Apparently, this time-warping thing had been practiced in secrecy with celebrities and others for years.

Real or not, we had nothing to lose, and humored Shelly. We all casually walked back out to the party as Jimbo said sternly, "There is zero room for errors. No one's going to fuck this up!" We all agreed to meet up early the next day, to set it all in motion. I made an early exit from the party. Knowing most of my stuff was still at Tiana's house, I found out she was going to be at her mom's late, and hurried over to the house.

Seeing Nalla again brought me warmth. "I missed you momma's". It felt good to be back here. This will always be my home. I gathered the last few items we needed from the closet and noticed a few blankets over a box I didn't recall seeing before.

It had writing on the top of the box that said, "For Mr. Marc McCray." Curious, I pulled the box out and opened it. Inside I found random documents and miscellaneous stuff from my dad. A manila folder stood out and I opened it.

It was a newspaper article with a title caption, "Toddler falls twelve stories, and walks away unscathed. Says a young boy caught him." *What the hell?* I wondered. *This story sounds very familiar. Yes, I remember now. I heard my mom talking about this story. Ever since I was a kid, I have heard this, and I always joked about it as I got older.*

"Oh yes, it's true, honey. In fact, I think your dad has an article about it somewhere," Mom told me when I asked about it one time

*Mom you really weren't shitting me all these years. Here it is, in my hands.*

"'A little boy caught me,' toddler told father after falling twelve stories." I continued to read: "A father, from San Diego, witnessed son fall twelve stories, only to find the young boy sitting at the bottom of stairs, unharmed told father a young boy jumped and caught him."

Reading this is simply unbelievable. Never believe everything in the paper, I have always said. Exactly how my dad's box ever got here, I'll never know. Something about this article gripped me, though, and I wanted to read more. I read on and heard a knock at the front door. I put the article in my shirt pocket, and peeked through the curtains and saw a native boy.

*What's a kid doing here at this time?* I thought.

*Oh shit! It's 7:20 p.m., dammit! What am I doing, wasting time here? Tiana and Taylor will be back from her mom's soon.*

I looked back through the window again and the boy was gone. *How weird is that?* I thought.

I didn't have time for any of this. I rushed out the door.

I got home and called Jim, with Shelly on the other line. After a little negotiating, it

was set. It would be for this Monday, with the three of us, at ten a.m. Operation M-Three-Ten was born, and I was the designated getaway driver.

# 13
## BREATHE

I HAD EVERYTHING in place and ready to go for the next day. I got in bed and called it a night. While in bed, trying to unwind, it was hard not to think of everything that was to come. I kept going over it all in my head. I turned on the TV to help me doze off.

*Bzzz! Bzzz! Bzzz!* I woke to the sound of my alarm clock and hit the snooze button. "Shit!" I yelled, remembering what day it was. Already behind schedule, Jim called my cell. I answered and said, "Hey man, yeah, I'm about ready."

Jim replied, "Meet at Bell Bros. coffee shop parking lot on 52nd St. at 8:45 a.m. Oh, and Caleb? I'm going to say this one more time. Don't fuck me!"

"Hey, I got it. Why the hell would I? I have just as much to lose as you do. In fact, I have more. It's my family. I said I'm in!"

He hung up.

Later that morning, we all met at Bell Bros. coffee shop and went over the details to perfect our plan. Shelly and Jim seemed eager and ready to go. I, however, was not. A gut feeling told me I needed to back out now. Knowing, however, that this was the only way to get my family back was what pushed me onward. There was no turning back.

With everything in place, we headed to the bank. The plan was to have Shelly close by, on watch, and to be a distraction in case something went wrong. I would wait in the car.

It was 10:03 a.m. on a clear Monday morning, and to my sur-prise the bank wasn't busy as we pulled up to the front of the bank. All I could think about were Tiana and Taylor. *This is for them!*

"Listen, Caleb, no matter what, do not panic, and do not leave this spot! You just wait here for me. This won't take long. Do not fuck this up!" said Jim.

Those words, and that look he gave me, hit me hard. I knew I could not be the weak link. I could not crack.

"You hear me? You're good?"

"Yes, of course. I'm good."

Jim loaded his pistols and headed inside.

*Deep breath and relax, you're good, Caleb, it will all be over soon. Just breathe.*

There I sat and waited for what seemed like an eternity.

I started sweating.

I leaned back while lighting up a cigarette, and noticed the time. I started to get antsy. I looked all around, with a feeling of being watched, as I tried to play it cool. Sweat began to drip from my forehead, and I became jittery. My knee bounced uncontrol-lably as I frantically looked all around me.

Bzzzz! Bzzzz! Bzzzz! Startled, I jumped back in my seat, real-izing it was my cellphone

vibrating next to me. I ignored it, and kept my eyes glued to the bank's front doors.

*Shit!* I thought, as I noticed a man staring right at me. Panic started setting in, as the continuous thoughts of the what-ifs plagued my mind. *What the hell?* I thought, as I heard a woman scream inside the bank. I looked to the entrance, and could not see anything through the

heavy, tinted-glass doors. More screams erupted from inside as passersby hear it and ran away.

*This is not good, where is he?* I thought. Paranoia began to set in as I realized something had to be wrong. We were running out of time!

All I could think about were Jim's last words, before he went inside: "Listen, Caleb, no matter what, do not panic, and do not leave this spot! You just wait here for me. This won't take long. Do not fuck this up!"

And then I heard it. *Bam! Bam!* Two shots rang out from inside. My heart skipped a beat.

*Oh shit! Shit! Don't leave. Don't leave!*

I slumped in my seat and peeked out of the driver-side window. This feeling of total helplessness had become too much to bear.

People began to look in my direction, and others began to stare. I couldn't take much more.

That's when I saw them. *No!* I thought in disgust. It was a woman and her little boy, walking toward the bank's entrance, clueless. Seeing that little boy as he looked up and smiled at his mother really got to me. That innocent boy's life could end on a day I would be part of?

*Hell no!* It changed everything, instantly.

My mind went blank to see they were now only a few feet away.

"Shit! Shit!" I panicked.

Just as the mother reached for the bank's door handle, as loud as I could I yelled, "Bomb! There's a bomb! Run!"

The woman grabbed her child and ran as the others scattered in hysteria. I started the car, knowing Jim would run out any second. I was ready to make our escape.

Seconds felt like minutes. I zoned out. Fear drew blood from my nose. I was completely paralyzed as chaos erupted around me. Even more people stared, as another person started to point at me. There were screams, the time, and just like that there was silence.

It was as if someone hit the pause button on a movie.

With it all becoming too much, I didn't even think twice. I gunned it.

With a gut-wrenching feeling in my stomach, I slammed the gas pedal and peeled out. All I could hear was the loud screech of my tires spinning out from behind me as I sped away.

I looked in the rearview mirror and swallowed my stomach. There was Jim. I couldn't believe it. Jim ran out into the middle of the street as he looked all around and saw me.

"Shit!" I yelled. Jim saw, as he pointed right at me, as I drove away. "No! No!" I yelled.

Sirens echoed all around, as dozens of police cars swarmed the area behind me. Jim was completely surrounded. "Oh no! No! What have I done?" I yelled, as I looked away in disgust.

*Turn back! No, keep going!* I told myself. Tears rolled down my face as I hit my steering wheel. I slammed the gas again, and continued to drive away. I know I was spotted by others, and even worse, I was guilty by association with Jim.

I was now a wanted man.

I couldn't go back. All I could think of were my wife and daughter. *I have to be free for them!*

*Where am I going to go now? I just need to get somewhere until this all blows over.*

I didn't have time to figure anything out. All I knew was, I had to get away. "You piece of shit! Fuck!" I yelled, as I slammed my fist on the center console.

I thought of Shelly. *Yes!*

I grabbed my phone and called Shelly, she didn't answered. Street after street I drove, passing tall buildings and cars with the fading sounds of sirens in the distance. My stomach was in knots, and I became lightheaded as I headed toward the

outskirts of town. I was dizzy and nauseous and I couldn't stop it. I threw up, everywhere. The damn smell was so bad. I looked down and saw it was all over my arms and in the floor-board. I didn't even care.

All I could think about was my little girl, Taylor, and Tiana. I wanted to see them so badly. I needed them!

As I proceeded driving to nowhere-land, I noticed a warning sign ahead for a sharp turn followed by a large wall. I picked up my phone and called Tiana but she didn't answer.

That was when it all hit me. I wouldn't answer me, either. I failed everyone. And I failed my family, most of all. Like the last few grains of sand slipping away through an hourglass, it was over. It was time to say goodbye.

I called Tiana again. "Caleb?" I heard.

"Tiana?" I replied.

Hearing her voice brought me instant calm. I said, "Listen, Tiana, you there?" as the connection got staticky. "Tiana!" I yelled again. The sounds of sirens become louder and closer. I began to fade, and blocked everything out.

A desperate urge to cry out overcame me. I just wanted to plead to whoever, or whatever, was out there. From the depths of my soul, and as loud as I could, I cried out, "God, please! Someone help me!"

Unsure if Tiana could hear or not, I hung up. I knew my life insurance policy and my mom would take care of them.

"You selfish piece of shit! You're trash! You have been in their way since day one! They deserve so much better than you. They deserve better than this... I hate you!"

I gripped the steering wheel, closed my eyes, and accelerated toward the wall ahead.

Intense heat covered my body. My life flashed before my eyes.

The impact I anticipated never came, and I heard only silence. I jolted and opened my eyes and couldn't believe it. Within in seconds from the wall, I saw someone walking in front of it. "Oh fuck!" I yelled while I yanked the wheel. To prevent hitting the man, I veered off the road toward a tree.

I sideswiped the tree, hitting my head on the steering wheel and car door. "Uh…my head," I muttered in pain while trying to regain myself. Blood covered my hands and shirt. *Oh no, that man!* I remembered as I come to. I looked back to the wall behind me and didn't see him. I backed the banged-up car, still running, and drove over to where I'd hit him.

*Oh God, I killed him,* I thought. I pulled over to the wall and got out for a closer look. "Oh shit! Are you okay?" I yelled out when I saw a young man in a construction pothole.

"Help! Down here!" The man yelled.

"Hold on! You're going to be okay," I replied.

I grabbed his arms, pulling him up to safety. "Are you okay? I'm so sorry. I hit you, are you okay?"

"Yeah, I'm all right. I'm not hit. Are you good?"

"Just shaken up some, but I'm okay. How are you not hit? I know I hit you."

I could see scrapes and cuts all over this guy, but to my surprise he appeared to be okay.

"What the hell are you thinking, walking so close to the highway like that? Are you crazy?" I asked the man.

The young man responded, "Crazy? Nah, not yet. I gotta say, though, I wasn't the one going 200 around this curve here right towards a wall." The young man asked, in a thick Latin accent, "Did your brakes go out? Or you've been drinking? I know it's one of the two."

Before I could answer, the man said, "Damn, man, you would have thought you were trying to kill yourself or something…" followed by a chuckle.

I grinned, replying, "Yes, actually. I was trying to do exactly that."

The young man laughed and ceased his laughter when he noticed my face was serious. "Ha! Ah, c'mon, man. That is funny, though.

I'm Maximino. Maximino Montez, Jr. You can just call me Jr."

I replied, "I'm Caleb McCray. It's nice to meet you, Jr. Standing here on the side of the road is not ideal I know. Wish it would have been better circumstances."

*What was it about this guy that drew my interest?* From that point, we continued talking, and I felt as if I knew him. I was curious to know more about this Max and asked, "You're not from around here, are you?"

Jr. responded, "Nope, we just moved here a few weeks ago. I must say, though, if this is how people drive here, I'm moving back." He laughed. Jr. continued, "Yeah, man, my family and I just came here from Portugal."

"Portugal? You're kidding?"

"Yeah, bro. My dad wanted us to see other cultures and for us to share ours, while bringing a message of good."

"A message of good? Don't tell me you're some kind of fanatic group?"

"Fanatic group? What's that?"

"Never mind."

"Nah, I'm just a messenger of positive and good of my heritage, from another place. You know, I represent my home, and where I come from. How you say it here? Em-bayssi-der?"

I laughed and replied, "Oh, you mean Ambassador?"

"Yes! That's it. Or as we call it back at home, an Embaixador."

"Ah, I see. That's pretty neat. Well, I'm part Irish. Well, Scottish-Irish. Sorry, I'm still in shock over how I missed you. I'm just glad you're okay."

"Caleb?" said Jr.

"Yeah?" I replied.

"Can we stop with this acting now?"

"Acting? I'm sorry, do I know you?"

"Of course you do. We know each other well. In fact, we're brothers from way before this. C'mon Caleb, you know this. You know why I'm here."

"Oh yeah? Brothers, huh? Okay, why are you here?"

*Unbelievable! Another lunatic? I'm trying to end this misery and there still drawn to me.*

"I'm here, to save you. Or bail you out. As you asked."

My jaw hit the floor. He proceeded to tell me he was here to remind me of who I really am, and that were both from another time. He said he was upset I tried to give up when I'm a badass with superior powers.

I wasn't sure what the hell all of that meant. All I could do was laugh.

Jr. did not laugh. He said, in order for me to see this, I first need to look past all the distractions around me in this system here and remove the scale-like blinders over my eyes, or "deceptors," he called them. Only then would I come to realize who I really am, and unlock my true potential.

What he said next really got me. Jr. said I was a target and a hit had been placed on me, and I was his new assignment to stop it. He was my protector, he said, and this time he would not fail.

*This guy and Shelly should hook up,* I thought. As I did with Shelly, I humored him. I knew this guy was nuts, capable of any-thing, and played it cool.

"Man, that's crazy. Just curious, how much is the bounty on me? Ahh, never mind. I'm just going to make this easy for them. I really was trying to end it. So, they can take me off their list," I said.

"I know damn it. That's why I'm here. I cannot tell you how

shocked I am. It's not like you to give up. We don't do that. You never give up," replied Jr. and shook his head.

While Jr. and I continued talking, I heard sirens in the distance. *Not good*, I thought. It was time to make an exit.

I said, "I see. That's pretty neat. Well, listen, I have to get going. Glad you're okay and nice to meet you. Take care, Max."

"Okay, Caleb, you know how much I hate this roll playing part of it. Fine, I'll play along. You know I'm going to get you back for this back home when this is over," Jr. said.

What? I'm so done with this guy. I told him that's fine and thanked him.

I headed over to my car and heard Jr. yell out, "Hey, Rapaz Bonito! You mind if I catch a lift back to my house just up the road? We can repair your bumper, too."

Puzzled, I asked, "Rapaz Bonito? Bumper? What the hell are you talking about now?"

"You saved me, man, and I owe you. I noticed your bumper looks bad, there, and my brother does body work; he can fix it for free for your troubles. And Rapaz Bonito; that's what I'll call you. It means 'pretty boy' in Portuguese. A man who drives a nice car like this and dresses like that, you know he has it together for the ladies."

I rethought this. *Before I say goodbye to this life, I might as well have a little fun. I have nothing to lose, literally.* Realizing I had nowhere to go, I accepted his offer.

"Estrondo!" Jr. yelled as I looked at him, confused. "Estrondo means, like, boom!"

I nodded with a grin, saying, "Got it." Jr. said, "We don't have many friends or visitors yet, since we're new, so my family would love to meet you."

We hopped in the car and headed over to Max Jr.'s place.

# 14

# A WARM PLACE

THROUGH THICK TREES and down a few winding dirt roads we headed to Jr.'s. On the way, I was digging his personality. In spite of his wild, incoherent talk, he had a good sense of humor. Hearing him try to make out some words with his accent was pretty funny.

Behind tall trees, in the distance, I could see a big, old secluded house and it hit me. *We're all kind of crazy, I know, but what if this guy is some sort of freak? Now, I'm going to go in his house to whatever or whoever else is in there?*

I was starting to get very uncomfortable. *Wait*, I further thought, *didn't I just try to end my own life just now? If someone else does it for me, that's all the better. He's probably on his way out, like me.* Whatever fear and concerns I had vanished as we pulled up through the driveway and headed into the big house.

"Well, this is it," Jr. said, "our humble casa."

"So, it's just you and your brother and sister living here, you said?"

Jr. looked at me, laughing, and replied, "C'mon, you know I brought the whole crew with me."

"Huh?"

"Oh yeah. My mistake. Err, um, actually, you mean me and my fourteen brothers and sisters and my father live here."

*Did he just say fourteen? What the shit?*

"Fourteen?" I asked.

Jr. nodded, saying, "Yup, I did. Fourteen of us plus my dad." We walked into the house.

When I walked inside, I was thrown back. We were greeted by many people, and what was odd was that they also treated me as if they already knew me. Is this some sort of acting school?

Max Jr. winked at everyone and whispered, "Just follow my lead," and the others faintly laughed.

*Follow my lead?*

"Everyone, this is Caleb Mc—uh—Caleb McCrary. Rapaz Bonito," Jr. said as the room filled with laughter. I responded "Hello, everyone. You mean McCray, not McCrary." I laughed. "McCray, oh yeah, I was just messing with ya, bro. I knew that. I'll show you around."

Max Jr. gave me a tour of the huge house and I was surprised how orderly and respectful they all were. *Don't any of them work? How they can all live here?* I wondered. "Estrondo! Just in time for dinner. I'm starved!" Jr. said.

We all gathered around the long dinner table and ate. Everyone was laughing and smiling through the idle conversations. *This is pretty neat,* I thought. For once, something felt good, even if it was only for a moment.

Noticing not all fourteen siblings or the father were there, I asked, "So, where's the others and your Dad?"

Kyra replied, "Oh, they work odd hours and days. My dad is a truck driver, so he travels with his work. In fact, when he was in town last, he said he ran into you at the store. He's the older-looking man who wears a grey fedora with a white feather sticking out, and tan khaki pants? I mean, you can't forget an old school guy like him. He always wears that same fedora hat, and khaki pants."

I replied, "He ran into me?"

Kyra replied, "Yes. He said he met a nice young man who helped him get a bottle of honey down from the top shelf. He said the young man was named Caleb and drove a nice car. I'm gonna say that was you? He said he felt a connection with you, and he would love to talk with you again.

"He said he had something to share with you. He will be back soon. I'm Max's sister Kyra, by the way," the young girl said.

"Well, it's a pleasure meeting you, Kyra. I'm Caleb. And, oh, wow! Yes, I do remember him! That's your father? He was pretty funny, actually. I could tell he doesn't get out much. Yes, I look forward to talking with him again."

I couldn't believe how fairly young they all were, and yet so mature. They had to be between fifteen and twenty-five.

Three others walked in, and for some reason they stared at me as if they didn't want me there for a second, as if analyzing me. I looked at Jr., who gave them a nod of assurance and said, "Yes, everyone, this is Caleb, my good friend. He actually saved me from falling into a big pothole. I could have died."

Everyone cheered and thanked me as Jr. said, "Yes, Caleb, we welcome you! As I said, our family is not small, so I'll give you the short version."

I laughed as Jr. continued, "This is our family; that's the eldest, the sneaky Michael. And the always determined Kyra, who you met, the acrobat. Here is my bro. Arron, the confident one, and there is Ciara, the meek.

And my other sister, Kalynn. She's the one with a big heart and the rock of the family.

Kalynn, with a big smile, said, "It's good to see you again, Caleb. I mean, it's good to meet you," followed with a chuckle.

Jr. laughed and continued, saying, "And there's my other little brother, Camden, our fighter, and a hell of a wrestler. And the always competitive Logan. He runs the family repair shop. The lovely Mia here, who's a heck of an overachiever. She has never met a mirror she didn't like."

"Oh no, she's ugly," Jaden said.

"And that's Jaden, my other brother with brute strength and the jokester, as you can see. Jaden is always great for a laugh. If you're feeling down, he will find a way to pick you up.

Gavin here, the fearless one. Over there is Avary, the nifty gadget girl. And the mini-pack, Brooklyn, the little servant. Standing next to you is Brenden, the highly intelligent, tech savvy one. His young age is misleading, he's well ahead of most. And the youngest, Liam. The tough little protector of the bunch."

After meeting everyone, we hung out and talked a while. Logan walked in from the garage and said, "Well, it's going to take a bit to fix that bumper. I'll get it done as fast as possible."

We sat at the dining table and the aroma of the food being served was a familiar one. The girls placed big platters on the table with steam coming off the lids. When the lids were removed, I was delighted to see homemade chicken enchiladas. Ironically, my favorite.

Jr. said, "Again, thanks for saving me. I owe you big time."

"No, you don't owe me anything. We're good, man," I replied.

Kyra said, "Well, sorry. Our English is not so good yet, as you can see. My dad speaks better English and he would love to talk to you. He's very knowledgeable about almost anything, really. I know he can really help you with whatever you're going through."

"Thank you. That's pretty cool, having a dad like that. I really will keep that in mind.

I felt as if I was right at home.

I began to wonder, *Why are these people being so warm to me? This entire day, in fact. All of it is so bizarre and doesn't seem real.*

I was ready to wake up from this nightmare, if that's what it was.

I just wanted them, or someone, to put me out of my misery.

# 15

## NEWS FLASH

"WELL, IT WAS banged up pretty good and now it's close to new. I think I got you all set, bro. Oh, and don't worry about the charges. I put it all on Jr.," Logan said. Everyone laughed.

In the next room I heard static from the TV.

"We interrupt this program for an emergency newsflash. At approximately 10:05 this morning, a bank robbery has been reported with at least two suspects.

"One of the suspect's seen here in this security footage clip wearing a grey ski mask and a blue hat, who initially got away, has been caught. James Thomas Barnes is believed to be the one in the security footage. The whereabouts of the second suspect is—" The others, from the other rooms, walked in as everyone listened closely to the TV.

*They caught Jim? Oh shit!*

I had to stop the newsflash and fast. I needed a diversion. I noticed a table lamp to my left and subtly knocked it over.

*Crash!* Everyone looked over, startled, and I said, "Oh, dammit! I'm so sorry, my fault."

I stepped on the glass as if I didn't see it, making more noise.

"We have reason to believe the second suspect is still in the—" the TV continued to say.

Michael added, "Eh, it's just a lamp. No worries, man."

Jr. yelled, "Turn it off!"

Now was the time to make my exit. I acted as if I had received an emergency text and had to go now, and said, "Well, I must be going now. Thanks so much again for dinner, and thanks for fixing my car, Logan. Jr., you're one cool dude. Thanks."

I walked out to my car and started to drive off. I heard "Caleb!" as I pulled away. I looked back and saw Jr. running toward me for some reason. "Caleb, hold up!" Jr. called out.

Jr. ran right in front of the car, forcing me to slam the brakes.

"What the hell are you doing? Me hitting you once today isn't enough?" I yelled. Jr. replied, "Real quick. My brother said that you never talked about the cost for fixing your car."

Confused, I said, "Cost? Wait a second, I thought you and your brother said there was no charge. That's fine, though. How much do I owe you?"

Jr. replied, "You're right, I did say no currency. I was kind of hoping you could help me out with a little favor. Since I'm new around here, with no job yet, and my old man will be gone for a few days, it gave me an ideal."

"Idea, you mean. It's 'idea.'"

Jr. laughed, saying, "Oh yeah. Idea. Since you're coming back here to meet my old man, I thought I could tag along? At least catch a ride in town?"

I couldn't believe I was even entertaining this silliness. However, he was harmless, and his wackiness was entertaining. I could also use a little company before I went into hiding. And at this point, what difference would it make? I actually liked the kid.

"Fuck it! Hop in," I told Jr.

"Excelente!" Jr. yelled with excitement and got in the car.

"Don't tell me. You're saying 'excellent' in Portuguese, right?"

"Correct," Jr. Replied.

I tuned, "In the air tonight" on the radio and we drove off into the sunset.

# 16

## ROLL OUT

DOWN THE DUSTY road toward the highway we went, and I actually started feeling good, with Jr. tagging along as he kept me company. I simply drove away to the unknown, without a care in the world. I could go wherever I wanted or do anything I wanted. I was already mentally gone from this world and reality. I knew in a few days none of this would matter.

Suddenly I felt like a heavy weight was on my chest and started to get antsy. Knowing I already unsubscribed here in this life, I wanted to open up to Jr. so that he could relay it. I knew it wouldn't make a difference if I did or not. I decided to tell Jr. Everything before I moved on, before I left this world.

I wanted nothing on me from this life. I was leaving it all here. Even though I already told him, even though somehow, he already knew, I'm going to tell Jr. exactly what I'm planning to do.

Jr. asked, "So where are we going?"

I looked at him with a slight grin and replied, "Who cares?

I know you don't have to work tomorrow. And you know what? Neither do I." We laughed.

"Good point," Jr. replied.

I was good all the way around. I had made my peace with Tiana and Taylor, knowing they would be taken care of. Jim was locked up, and I was about to make peace with myself, by opening up to some random kid I didn't even know. Although he claimed to know me and was my guardian of sorts, which was pretty comical.

Knowing I was already dead to Tiana and my little girl, and to everyone else, for that matter, made it all the easier. There was no going back to what had been. It was time to clean out this old closet one last time.

I continued telling Jr. everything, from how life was golden, to sudden issues starting at work. The cheating, the money, and the marriage problems and the car accident. How it all added up to losing my family. I even told Jr. how I lost my father at a young age, which still has an effect on me to this day.

The failed bank heist, however, will be the only thing I'm going to take with me when I leave here.

I told him I simply ran out of gas on this ride of life we are all on, and I didn't want any more of it. Everyone would be so much better off if I was gone. I wanted out.

Jr. looked at me with a raised eyebrow and said, "Really? C'mon, bro, this is silly. You know you're better than this drama shit. This is not you."

He quickly gathered himself and added, "Damn it! Sorry, I forgot again. I meant, no way! Never think like that! All you need to do is talk to someone. You should talk to my dad. He's good about stuff like this, and helped so many back home. He can help you!"

"Max, are you kidding me? This is not a fucking joke! This is my life! I think you can stop with the bullshit already. As cool as your dad is, I'm going to decline. It's too late for all that, I'm done. At the end of the day, I can honestly say I would have been better off if I had never existed."

"Hey, listen, bro. We're not going there. God doesn't make mistakes. It does not have to be this way. Think of your little girl! She depends on you! She needs you!"

I said, "I know she does. That's why I'm doing this. Tiana and Taylor need money right now in the worst way. I fucked their future and lives up. It's all because of me. And I will not be the one on their minds, knowing it was all because of me as they grow old. Not when I can at least fix it. My family will get enough from my life insurance policy. They will be okay."

"So, this is all about money?" Jr asked.

"Yeah, that's exactly what this is about. Why do you say it like that? Are you telling me that you got that money thing down and can help or something? You got it all figured out for me? You have the money I need?"

"You don't need that shit." Jr. caught himself, "I mean, no. Sorry, I don't."

"Exactly! No one knows what I'm going through! No one! So please, let's just enjoy the little time I have left here and let's make the best of it. Sorry. I don't mean to come off a short. I know you did not mean it like that.

When I say goodbye to you and to this world, none of this will matter in the least anymore. I won't matter, nor will I care."

Jr. started to say something and I quickly interrupted him. I said, "Ok, that's enough. Listen to me. If you really do want to help me like you claim you do. You say you owe me a debt, right? Okay, fine. Here's how you can settle it.

"From here onward, don't ask any more questions. All you have to do is relax and don't piss me off. That's the only help I want. Or, I can drop you off right here and you can hitch back. You got it?"

I couldn't tell, really, as it seemed Jr. was a little teary-eyed as he nodded. I was not in the mood for any mushy shit, and I knew it was time to change this tune. I asked, "So what kind of fun do they have in Portugal?"

Jr. looked up at me, confused.

"I have a little time to kill, and you wanted me to show you around the town, right? Well, that's exactly what I'm going to do. And the best part of it all, is that it's all on me."

Max Jr. slowly started shaking his head no. I added, "All you have to do is sit back, and go with it all for a few days of carefree fun. Again, if it's too hard for you, I have no problem dropping you off at this very moment. I'll be on my marry way.

"As my last request, however, before I leave this earth, I would like to enjoy my remaining time here with someone. There's nothing you can do to stop it, so please just accept it. So what do you say, Mr. Maximino Jr.? You coming or not?"

Jr. reluctantly replied, "Yes, I'm in."

"Nice! That's my boy. I appreciate you lending an ear, but enough of all this mushy mumbo jumbo bullshit! Are you ready to party or what?"

Jr. replied, "Uh, sure. What did you have in mind?"

With a sly grin, I asked, "Feeling lucky? We're going to start at a place where whatever should happen there, will always stay there. And I'm not talking Vegas. This place is better. Just sit back, little Jr., and enjoy the ride."

# 17

# PAINTING THE TOWN

O FF WE WENT through the streets of beautiful downtown San Diego. From the gorgeous palm trees, to the smell of sea salt from the ocean, it was truly a sight. Jr. had never been to this side of town, to my surprise. He was amazed how different everything looked.

"Okay so what's this place that's so great?" Jr. asked.

I replied, "It's called BL's. It's a club I like to go to get my mind of things."

"A club? What do you mean club? Like a stick?"

"This is a club," I replied as we pulled up to the valet of BL's. We got out and I noticed Jr. was totally speechless. "Jr., welcome to BabeLand's." We went inside.

Flashy cars, bright lights, and naked women were everywhere. Of course, I was immediately treated like royalty. "Mr. McCray, welcome back. Would you like your normal everything?" Marty, the club manager, asked.

"Absolutely! This is Max, by the way, my good buddy."

Marty greeted Jr. and led us to my normal VIP spot, where we were showered with girls and champagne.

"Damn! You really are a Rapaz Bonito. These women here are more beautiful than the girls back home. Estrondo!" Jr. said with excitement.

I laughed and handed Jr. a glass of Champaign. "You drink, right?" I asked him.

He replied, "Uh…yeah, man, sometimes."

"A Toast to you, Jr., and to the family from Portugal. Welcome to America!"

Jr. smiled and thanked me as we drank together.

An hour or so went by and I could see Jr. seemed bothered about something. For some reason, Jr. kept staring hard at two guys at the other table. The two guys stared back. Maybe he knew them.

"Hey, man, you all right? Is something wrong?" I asked Jr.

He replied, "Yeah, I'm okay. Just not used to all this, I guess."

I ordered a round of shots, to loosen Jr. up.

"All right, gents, let's give it up for the sexy X'tacy to the main stage!" the DJ announced. "Damn! That X'tacy's ridiculous hot, right?" I asked Jr.

He didn't respond. He was staring at a corner, for some reason.

Out of the dark corner, a striking young man leaned into the light with an eerie smirk on his face. The peculiar man stared right at Jr., as if he knew him, while giving an almost sarcastic nod, and faded back into the darkness. "Who the hell was that?" I said. "You know that guy?"

Jr. looked all around, as if looking for someone. "Yes, I think so," Jr. replied.

Jr. continued to act uneasy, almost paranoid, and told me not to leave his side. He kept looking at me, and all around us. "We should leave, Caleb," he said. "It's a little too smoky in here, or something. Let's go check one of those other places you go to? It's too crowded in here for me."

I replied, "Yeah, maybe we will in a bit. I thought you were having a good time, though? I think you just need to loosen up a little is all." I handed him another drink and a shot.

Although reluctant at first, Jr. finally loosened up as we toasted the night. I laughed when Jr. said, "I'm feeling a little tipsy, no more for me." I could tell he was feeling pretty good, unable to take his eyes off the girls onstage.

*Is that that same man across the way who smirked at Jr. earlier?* I wondered. *Yes, it is!*

A group of girls surrounded him, and I noticed he handed one of the girls a few drinks and pointed in our direction. The girl casually walked over to us and as she got closer, I was completely mesmerized by her beauty. She was by far the sexiest and hottest girl in this place.

She was perfectly curved with long black shiny hair and gorgeous green eyes. That tan skin with luscious red lips made her irresistible. Damn. I wanted her.

"Hey there, boys…" the girl said with a seductive smile, holding three drinks. *Wow! How fine is this woman?* I thought. My night was about to go from good to damn good. What I saw this girl do next, however, floored me. "I'm Siy'ra. Would you like some company?"

"Uh…sure," Jr. hesitantly replied.

Siy'ra sat on his lap as they drank.

Within a matter of moments Siy'ra started rubbing up on Jr., giving him his first lap dance. Jr. looked at me, confused, unsure of what was happening. I gestured it was okay and gave him the thumbs up. Jr. leaned over to me and whispered, "Caleb, whatever you do, don't leave my sight, okay?"

I laughed and replied, "I won't, don't worry. Just go with it and relax."

With Jr.'s night now set; I also grabbed a girl, along with a few more drinks. The party was on.

"I'll be right back; I'm going to get a lap dance with that girl really quick, right over there," I told Jr., who looked at me and nodded.

I took the girl I was with to the VIP booth for a few dances. *Damn, these drinks are hitting me,* I thought as I stumbled on the way back to our table.

I got to our table and to my surprise Jr. was gone. *Maybe he went to the bathroom,* I thought, and waited. Loud music, hundreds of people, and smoke everywhere made it hard to focus. For nearly forty minutes I looked around and waited, and Jr. was nowhere to be seen.

"Hey man, here you go... I saw this fall out of your pocket just now." I turned around and it was that guy who was looking at Jr., who sent Siy'ra over. He was handing me my cellphone.

"Really? Well, shit. Thanks, man, I appreciate it."

The man smiled, shook my hand, and said, "Hey, I'm Dain Stone. You come here a lot?"

I replied, "From time to time. What's up man, I'm Caleb McCray. Stone, huh? Are you in porn or something? Sounds like a porn name." I laughed.

"Porn? I wish. They tell me that's my name because of how it matches me and my heart; hard as Stone, heart of Stone," He grinned. Dain added, "Actually, Stone is my middle name. Mirtaza is my last. Dain Stone Mirtaza."

We talked for a bit as Dain bought a few rounds of drinks. Dain was young and intimidating, standing about 6'3" or so. He was clean-cut and sharply dressed. He had a pompadour, with dark fifties gangster, yet gothic attire. I could see his ears were pierced and he had unique sleeve and neck tattoos. He was very confident and smooth.

"You come here a lot?" I asked.

"Nope. First time."

"First time? Nice. What brings you out on this special night?"
He replied, "You."

"Me?" I laughed. "Do I know you?".

"Oh, yes."

"I do? I don't think so. What do you want with me?"

"To kill you. As you asked."

Chills shot up my spine. Speechless, I watched him noncha-
lantly take another drink and chuckle. He casually pulled out
cash and threw at the dancer on the main stage. With a wink, he
handed me a wad of cash and a drink to join him.

I couldn't believe my ears. The room spun around me as I
watched his subtle grin.

*Is this guy for real? This drunk fuck!*

Enraged, I threw my glass at his face. I grabbed his head and
smashed it onto the stage, repeatedly.

No, that's not what happened. Oh, did I want to, though. I
was about to smash his face, I should say. However, my curiosity
got the best of me.

"What the hell did you say? Is that some kind of joke?" I said.

"How did you know that?"

"Max," Dain replied.

I cringed in disbelief.

"So, you're the supposed hitman that's after me?"

Dain laughed. "Yup. That's me." He handed me another drink.

I was frozen. *Is this really happening?* I thought.

I was drunk. *I'm not really hearing this right now.* I tried to get
it together. I felt off-balance and held onto the table.

Dain chuckled and helped me regain my balance. "Pardon
my sense of humor, it's a little dry. We're all just having a good
time here. To you," he said with a smile, and held up his drink.
He laughed. I laughed, and we toasted the night. He acted as if
nothing was ever said. Whatever was happening, this guy was

cool as shit. There was something about him. He had an alluring demeanor. *Obviously, Jr. knows him and had to have told him of me. It's clear this guy has a dark sense of humor.* I couldn't think. I took another drink and let it go.

There was still no sign of Jr. I wanted to ask Dain how he knew who Jr. was and what was up with that odd interaction between them earlier. I got distracted, however, as a group of Dain's girls joined us.

After we all downed another round of shots, I noticed the girl sitting on my lap pulled out her cellphone. She checked her texts, then browsed through news articles.

*What the hell?*

"I'm sorry, can I see your phone really quick?" I asked.

"Oh sure," replied the girl.

I read one of the articles and my heart stopped.

*The captured bank robber escaped?*

*Jim escaped! Oh, fuck! My family! He's going to go after them. If he couldn't find me, he would target and turn to Tiana and Taylor! He's going to seek revenge for bailing on him, and leaving him to his fate. He's going to kill my family!*

I grabbed my cell and realized it was dead! Dain noticed, and to my surprise, pulled out the right charger from his pocket. *Well, that was a little weird.* I plugged the charger in and powered it on. I saw many missed calls and texts from Tiana, family, and friends. Scrolling through the logs, I saw a missed call and three texts from a random, unsaved number.

I open the texts. It was Jim! "Yes, it's me. I'm free. I said not to fuck me, and you did. You pussy! Now you and your family are fucked. I don't have to know where you're at when I know exactly where your wife and daughter are. Fuck a getaway driver!"

*Oh shit! No!*

I fell out of my chair in shock. My heart started palpitating as I tried to digest what I'd just read.

"Hey man, you okay? What's wrong?" Dain asked.

"My family!" I replied.

I called Tiana and there was no answer. I tried again and it went to her voicemail.

*Where the fuck is Jr.?* I wondered. I felt for my keys in my pockets and they weren't there! "Oh fuck! Oh fuck!" I said, looking frantically around the table and the floor for my keys.

"My keys. I'm missing my keys, and I have to leave now!" I said.

Dain started looking all around for them. Neither of us could find them.

"Where did Jr. go? Did you see where he went?"

Dain replied, "Yeah, I thought you knew. He and that girl left a while ago together. He told me to tell you not to worry and that he would be back. Does he have your keys?"

"Do you have to leave? I have no problem giving you a ride, I was about to leave as well," Dain added.

I was confused as none of this added up. I just didn't have time to think. Dain apologized for taking some of his jokes too far and said he would help me. Worrying about Jr. was no longer my concern. I had to get to my family. With no other options, I accepted Dain's offer and we headed to my house, to Tiana and Taylor.

# 18
## DEAR JOHN ...

ON THE WAY home I called Tiana's cell over and over with no answer. It was almost two a.m. when we pulled up to my house and I noticed all the lights were on.

"Tiana! Tiana!" I yelled as I dashed through the front door. "No! Where are they?"

"Nalla!" I yelled, and noticed she was in the back yard.

Like a madman I searched the whole house. Tiana and Taylor were gone. *Maybe she went to her mothers for the night,* I thought. *What's that?* I noticed a letter pinned next to the front door with "To Caleb" on the front.

I opened the letter and read it, and when I did my worst nightmare came to pass. The letter read: "Hello Caleb. Just a happy returning customer of yours, here… Next time I know of anyone needing a good getaway driver for hire, I'll be sure to send them your way. Now enough of the bullshit! Yes, I have your precious wife and little girl."

My head was spinning. I couldn't believe it.

The letter continued: "Question is, how much are they really worth to you? How much are they worth to me? Oh, I'd say $80k worth. Well, a lot more than that, really. For you, however, I'm giving a great loyal friend discount. I told you not to fuck me and you did. Even still, I'm giving you a choice. It's $80k in 48 hours, or you won't see your family again. No one will. Meet me at Old Juniper square 222. McAndrews road. It's a secluded, old barn. Text when ready. PS: Fuck you!"

*I will kill that piece of shit!* I thought. I called Jim and he didn't answer. I texted Jim, saying I had the money and wanted to meet, now. It was 1:38 a.m. and he responded. He agreed to meet.

I didn't waste a second as I ran outside, where Dain was waiting, and stumbled down the stairs.

"Whoa! You all right? Take it easy, man, you're drunk. Is that your dog?" asked Dain.

I looked back and there was Nalla in the backyard, growling and barking at Dain through the side gate.

*She has never acted that way before to strangers,* I thought.

"Nalla, no!" I yelled.

Suddenly, Nalla jumped the gate and charged toward Dain.

Dain quickly got back into his car and shut the door as Nalla lunged at the window, snapping at him.

"Nalla! No! What the hell has gotten into you?" I yelled, as I picked her up and put her in the house.

"I'm sorry about that. Nalla never has acted that way before to anyone."

"It's okay, man. She probably smells my dogs on me," replied Dain.

"Listen, I need your help one more time. My family is in serious danger. Can you take me to another place?" I asked.

Being with a total stranger in this situation is unimaginable. But to have a total stranger help you save your family while drunk, is insane as hell. There was just no choice. Tiana and Taylor needed my help, and I quickly filled Dain in.

"I'm so sorry to hear all of that. I'm not sure what I walked into here and it's obviously deep," Dain said. *He's not going to help me,* I thought. "However, and against my better judgment, I will help you. Where's this place and what's the plan?"

We headed to Old Juniper Square, and I tried to focus on some sort of plan and couldn't. I had no plan, I had nowhere near the money he wanted, and I didn't even know what to expect. It was as if I was on autopilot and I was just going. On the way I told Dain I couldn't think and I really had no plan, and even worse, I didn't have the $80,000.

"What the fuck? Hold up. You're telling me that I'm getting involved in a dangerous ransom situation right now? You never said that shit," Dain said, worried.

"Listen, I will make it worth your trouble. Or at least just drop me off in the area," I pleaded.

"I have no clue why I'm even considering doing this. You're damn lucky that this is in line with my kind of business, and that I have been through this before. Besides, you're still shit faced and can barely talk and will fuck this up. Don't worry; I'm going to help you. We'll talk about that repayment later."

It all happened fast from there. Just like that, we were at Old Juniper Square, and I could see the red barn ahead.

The night was cold, dark, and rainy, giving off a creepy feeling. There I sat, staring at the raindrops that crashed down on the windshield, trying to grasp what was happening. We got closer, and there in the distance was Jim's car.

"Okay, I have a plan. All you have to do is stay low and not be seen and keep a lookout. If something goes wrong, take this..."

Dain loaded a pistol and handed it to me.

"Wait, just how the hell are you going to pull off the having no $80,000 part?" I asked.

Dain replied, "Just don't worry; I will take care of that."

Still trying to sober up, all I could do was nod while I hunched down, out of sight. Dain nodded while he pulled his black hoodie over his head, grabbed an umbrella, and got out of the car. He walked back and opened the trunk, put a black satchel on his shoulder, and grabbed a brown bag.

My heart palpitated and my palms were sweaty, as I watched Dain through the blur of the rain-soaked windshield as he walked toward Jim's car.

Jim got out with what looked like a gun and opened the back-passenger door. It was them! Tiana and Taylor got out, with Jim pointing the gun at them. I started to lose it and instantly wanted to run to them as I gripped Dain's gun. Somehow, I kept it together, staying in the car, not taking my eyes off them. There they stood, Jim and Dain, a short distance from each other in the rainy darkness.

Dain walked closer to Jim and stood there for what seemed like forever. The heavy rainfall made it too hard to make out what was said. "Stop right there!" I heard someone yell. It sounded like Jim. I saw Dain hand the brown bag to Jim. Jim opened the bag, looked inside, and closed it. Dain leaned close to Jim and appeared to whisper something in his ear.

What I saw next I could not believe. Jim simply handed Tiana and Taylor over to Dain, got into his car, and drove away. "Holy shit! He did it!" I yelled. I got out of the car, and ran toward them. "Tiana!".

"Oh my God! Caleb!" Tiana yelled, in tears.

I grabbed them both and hugged and kissed them tightly. "I thought I lost you! I have been hearing all these things," Tiana said, distraught. "What's happening? And who is this?"

I told Tiana Dain was a good friend of mine and that this was all a serious misunderstanding. I told Tiana she needed to stay at her mother's, while I took care of a few things. I opened the car door for Tiana and Taylor.

I walked to the back of the car, where Dain was putting his things back in the trunk and asked, "How the hell did do that? Did you really just hand him over $80,000?"

Dain replied, "It's all taken care of. He won't be an issue for you anymore."

"You're kidding! I can't even tell you how grateful and thankful I am! How much do I owe you?"

"We will figure that out later. Focus on your family, now. No need to worry, it's taken care of."

I was floored. I hopped in the backseat with Tiana and Taylor as Little Taylor smiled and kissed me and held my hand.

"Where are we headed to now?" asked Dain.

"Oh sorry, just keep going, I'll tell you," I replied.

On the way to Tiana's mother's house, I told Tiana I was in trouble. Distraught, Tiana insisted on calling the police. I told her not to call yet and assured them they were okay now, Taylor was safe.

"I have to go take care of something and I'll be back in a few days. Stay at your mom's until I come get you. I'll call you tonight and explain everything. Trust me, everything is okay now," I said.

"Just keep me posted," she said. "I'm very worried."

"Don't be. It's all okay, I promise."

I could see the confusion and worry on her face. I hated that I had to put her and Taylor through that. We drop off Tiana and Taylor safely at her mom's around 2:45 a.m. I told Dain, "Head back to the club. We have to go back for Max; he's just a kid and has no car. I'm hoping my keys were found. Can you call your friend Siy'ra?"

Dain said okay and tried calling Siy'ra, who didn't answer.

We got back to the club, which was closed. A few employees were walking out and I asked them if my keys were found. Surprisingly, someone did turn my keys in. I asked the two employees if they noticed a young Latin kid with a San Diego charger hat. They had no clue.

Maybe he found a ride home. Either way, Jr. was gone.

With Tiana and Taylor now safe, and Jr. gone, and I guess at home, I knew I had to stay away for a bit. The police will come looking for me. I just want to settle up with Dain, and get away.

"Thanks again for this, man. I can't tell you much this means to me. So how much do I owe you now?"

Dain replied, "So you need a place to stay for a few days to lay low? You can stay at my place with my other siblings until all blows over. Also, I think I can help you with your situation you have going on. C'mon, we can discuss all of that at my place, follow me."

His house? *I know Dain helped me and all, however, going to some stranger's house is not something I want to do. But, I know he helped me and saved my family, and I owe him money.* I felt obligated. And really, what else was I going to do? *I'll go to his place, settle up with him, and leave.*

"All right, that sounds good. Do you live far?" I asked. Dain said he didn't live far and with nothing to lose, off we went to Dain's house.

# 19

## A NEW FRIEND

THROUGH WINDING DIRT roads and thick trees, we drove up a hill to a three-story house. It reminded me of Jr.'s place. Only this house had a dark and sinister look to it. It was a black, old-fashioned house with no lights at all. The awnings looked exaggerated with what appeared to be claws over the windows. It was surrounded by a black gate made with bizarre shapes, and two leashed dogs in the yard, barking.

*That's weird. The dogs' bodies have all white fur and black heads?*

We got out of our cars and headed up the stairs, and I instantly felt my nose run. It was blood.

"Hey, your nose is bleeding. You all right?" Dain said. I told him I was fine.

The dogs lunged, barked, and snapped at me.

"Vex, Rue! No! Shut your ass's!" yelled Dain. "And those are my dogs. Rue, she's the one with one red eye and the other white. Vex, he's the one with yellow eye. Depending on his mood, his eyes changes to all black when he's upset. Weird, huh?"

"I've never seen dogs like them before. What kind of breed are they?"

"Cachorros Morto's. For some reason they bring great fear on people. I don't know why? There very mellow, actually."

*What?* I thought. *Damn psycho dogs.*

We got up the stairs and to my surprise I heard smooth, catchy music. It was very different, a type of slow grunge with minimal lyrics I couldn't understand. *I'm digging this music.* It sounded like there was a party going on inside.

"They're partying at almost four a.m.?" I said.

Dain replied, "Always."

*Always? Damn.*

Inside the house I was blown away how everything looked. It was almost 3D-like. There were sinister tapestries, statues, and paintings, and caged, unfamiliar creatures. I was unable to keep my eyes off the striking décor, as if it pulled me to it. The furniture were in the shapes of bizarre creatures. The statues, figures, and creatures, and the strange hieroglyphics and writings, were from another time.

I felt uneasy. *Maybe it's because I have never seen anything like that before,* I thought. The allure of all the dark and bluish coloring completely mesmerized me. *What the hell is this place?* I wondered.

I followed Dain through hallways and corridors of the dark mansion. I felt a gust through each room and an odd attractive aroma. It all gave off a creepy, yet curious feeling. "This way," Dain said as I followed him to the enormous living room. As I walked in the dimly lit room, mist filled the air. I saw many people, all of them familiar in appearance.

They were all young and good-looking, like models. They were gothic like, with an appealing, dark mystique about them.

*Are these people some kind of high-class gypsies?*

Like Dain, all of them were tatted up with some piercings with extremely cool clothes I had never seen before. They had subtle grins as they stared at me with looks that drew me into them while they drank and smoked joints. Over there, I saw a girl and a guy snort lines of another girl's stomach. *I can't believe I'm seeing this*, I thought. It was four a.m., and the partying showed no signs of stopping.

It was as if I'd walked into a dark, mist-filled, sinister night-club with strobe lighting. Everyone was laughing, while others shot up unknown drugs. Some of the women were topless and others naked as they danced to the sensual catchy music. They were unbelievably beautiful and sexy with a dark, alluring appeal.

I looked over at the couch and I saw a woman performing fellatio on someone. Another woman was on top of a man, gyrating and grinding, looking right at me as they moaned in pleasure. They were drawing me into them. *Damn, I love this. I want them!* I was dangerously curious, and I wanted it all. In spite of the appeal, however, I had an uneasy feeling and didn't feel right. Something told me to get out.

I turned to Dain, to tell him something had come up. I had to leave, but he was gone. Standing in his place were two half-naked, exotic women, both with wicked fuck-me-now smirks on their faces. They handed me a drink as they began to dance and grind on me, feeling me up all over. I became aroused and instantly felt powerless before their beauty and charm. I partook of an unknown drink that was handed to me as one of the girls pushed me onto the couch behind me. I was swarmed by other beautiful young women who kissed and caressed me all over.

A mist of smoke and sharp beams of light covered the dark room that was filled with laughter and celebration. The second-hand smoke of an unknown drug was exhaled into my mouth by another girl, followed by a sensual kiss. An intense feeling of arousal hit me like never before.

I was feeling good. I wasn't going anywhere. Out of the mist, Dain appeared.

"My family…" Dain said as the music and partying stopped. "This is my good friend Caleb. Caleb is our brother and our guest of honor," Dain added. Everyone clapped and cheered and made me feel right at home.

"Caleb, these are my brothers and sisters…" *Did he just say brothers and sisters?* I thought. *Like it's his real family? They can't be!*

"Caleb, these are my flesh and blood siblings, so you better watch your hands with my little sisters, there," Dain said with a sarcastic laugh.

*What the fuck? I'm in the midst of a freak show,* I thought.

Dain waved his arm, pointing at one of his brothers, sitting on the stairs, and said, "Caleb, this is my family…"

One of the young men said, "A pleasure. I'm Joxel, the sly eldest."

A girl standing next to him said, "I'm Zitaya, the haughty," and smirked.

Dain said, "Over there are my two brothers, Stadiel, the conceded shit and the gluttonous pig Gibborim. And there is my easy sister Zariall, who can't get enough. They laughed.

*Is this a joke? Am I freaking out from that drug I inhaled? Whatever it was, the crude humor these guys have is hilarious,* I thought.

Dain added, "And the envious Ithuriel, my sister, with my idolizing brother Humatiel. Next to you is my crafty witch sister Amitiel, my deadbeat sloth of a brother Rahmiel, and my drunk brother, Gadriel. That's the hateful Valoel, my sister, along with my depressed brother Kasbiel, who is on sui watch as they say." They laughed.

*What the hell kind of names are these?* I wondered.

Here next to me is Sorush, my brother who's wanted for murder, and my other rebel brother Jyrel. And, of course, you already met my sons, Vex and Rue, my dogs. Like I said, they really are sweet.

There was an awkward silence.

I looked around the room as they all returned blank stares.

*Hell no.* Joking or not, I wanted to leave. However, I was high and out of it. I knew I had to play it cool. I said, "It's a pleasure to meet everyone. I'm going to go on a limb here and say you guys are not from around here, right?"

Everyone laughed. Zitaya said "They're funny, huh? Here," and passed a joint to me. I looked at this mystery drug in my hand, unsure. Zitaya seductively gazed into my eyes and moved my hand to my mouth, and I took a hit; one... two... three... four...five and six. I held the hit and exhaled. I began to cough and my head became clouded.

"Of course we're not from around here. Now that you've met the family, it's time to sit back and enjoy the show," said Dain, as he emerged from the shadow. Instantly it hit me as everything came to a slow blur. I felt lightheaded and started hallucinating. Dain stood before me with an evil smirk and took a hit from a joint. He exhaled, blowing a puff of smoke toward me that turned into a demonic figure.

Like some great showman, Dain began performing magic. A blue, electric orb appeared out of nowhere on both of his out-stretched hands. Music and laughter rang louder and louder in my ears and everything seemed to be in slow motion. The misty room grew darker as Dain's sisters continued to fondle and lick me all over, talking to me in some other language.

*No! No!* I told myself, wanting it all to stop. I knew I had to get out of there. I wanted to go home to Tiana and Taylor. *Fuck all of this!* I tried to get up but one of the girls pushed me down, unzipped my pants, and began to perform fellatio on me. I was mentally drained, weak and powerless in every way. I closed my eyes, leaned back, and no longer resisted.

"Caleb...hey, man!" I heard someone yell next to me. I opened my eyes and saw daylight. I found myself sprawled out on a couch with drool all over my arm. I quickly recalled where I was and why I was there. *Settle with this guy, and get back to Tiana and Taylor,* I thought.

"How'd you sleep?" Dain asked.

"Okay, I guess. Oh, I feel like shit. Where did everyone go?"

"They crashed out upstairs somewhere. Yeah, last night was pretty wild. You hit it hard."

I started to recall some of the night and I was still trying to comprehend it all.

"That magic and stuff you were doing last night? That was some hardcore trippy shit you did. What the hell was that? Are you some kind of sorcerer?"

Dain laughed and replied, "Maybe…" with a smirk. "What did you see? I remember showing you a few little basic tricks and stuff. I'm pretty sure what you saw had a lot to do with what you smoked." He laughed.

"I don't know. Whatever it was, hallucination or not, it all seemed damn real," I replied.

I thanked Dain for the offer to stay a few days. I told him I was good though, and I really needed to get back home to my wife and daughter. I asked him again about repayment. To my surprise, he said not to worry about it.

*Don't worry about it? Is this guy for real?*

I was blown away and so grateful when I heard that. I felt compelled to open up to him a little more before I left.

I told him of my problems back at home, with work, and how I lost family through a severe financial crisis. Dain was sympathetic, hearing my issues and hardships, and I could see he was concerned. It was as if he understood me.

*Is this the same person I was with yesterday?* I wondered.

"Your family is being destroyed? Oh yes, don't worry. I'm going to help you with that," said Dain.

I told Dain to pardon my skepticism, but I knew he couldn't help me. Dain looked at me and said, "Oh, I can help you, and I will. In fact, the next time you and Tiana see each other, it will all be different. For now, though, we're going to chill one last night, and I'm going to help ease your mind."

*He's going to save my family again? How can he say these things? Who is this guy?* I wondered.

Dain added, "Consider this a part of your repayment. Call your wife and check on them. Let her know all is well and you will be home tomorrow."

What was it about him? He had a very smooth way and carried himself well. He was convincing and made me feel so comfortable. I don't know why, but I did just that.

I called and checked on Tiana and Taylor and they were safe. I assured her everything was okay and to have her mom take her home tomorrow and I would be there. She cried and insisted I come now and that she was scared. I reassured her that it was all going to be okay and I had to do this. I told her to be strong for Taylor, and that I loved her and would see her tomorrow.

I hated hanging up with her that way, but I had no choice. I knew she and Taylor needed me.

"Now, if you thought last night was a good time, wait until you see tonight," said Dain.

I looked at Dain, thinking, *a good time? Oh no, I don't want to do more of that shit! And how the hell can any party get as wild and crazy as last night?*

It could and did. We all went to exclusive, hidden under-clubs that were simply mind-blowing.

Club to club we went, and I had never seen anything like these places. Everything was in abundance and handed out freely. Anything we desired was at our disposal. Alcoholic drinks, drugs, and food of all kinds were everywhere. I looked across the way and saw, in the next room, naked women and men having an orgy.

Through the smoke, I could see Dain standing in front of me as he directed traffic: who was to go where, or do what. With a wave of his arm, he sent three girls to me, who handed me an unknown joint and a drink.

I didn't feel right, I did not want anymore. I was stuck.

One of the girls straddled me and started grinding on me, as the other two kissed and fondled me all over. I looked at Dain, who gave a nod and a wicked grin.

Everywhere we went, people threw themselves at Dain as if he was some kind of rock star. As the night progressed, in these dark and hidden many places, it was easy to see Dain was like a god.

# 20
## ROUND ONE

T HAT NEXT DAY, while trying to recover again from yet another wild night, I thanked Dain. I told him I couldn't thank him enough for having me and for all he had done for me and my family. "It's all my pleasure, man. I think you're pretty cool and could tell there was something about you, different perhaps from all the others," Dain said.

This mysterious house, Dain's odd family, those parties, and what he'd done for me were all so overwhelming and hard to comprehend. I was intrigued, and wanted to know more about Dain.

"So, do all of your siblings live here? Where do they all work? This is all so, well, different to me."

Dain replied, "Differently cool, right?"

I said "Do you know Jr.'s family as well? It's so crazy that you both have a large family. How does one meet two big families within a week?"

"Yes, all my siblings do work, and they all live here. And, oh yes, I do know Jr.'s family well. Speaking of your friend there…"

I replied, "Yes, Jr., it's really bothering me not knowing if he is okay and if he made it home the other night. I'm going to check on him when I get home. Again, thanks for everything. I better head back."

Dain hesitantly replied, "Of course. Before you go, I think you should know something of what I was trying to say about your friend Jr. there. I hate to even tell you this. You may want to keep your guard up and watch it when you're around him."

"What the hell are you talking about?"

"I have a close buddy that was with us the other night at the club, who hung out with Max Jr. after we left. Later that night, my buddy said Max Jr. was bragging about how he was with Siy'ra, taking her to a hotel.

"And at that hotel, Jr. raped and beat Siy'ra pretty bad."

I was dumbfounded. I said, "No way! Is she okay? Your buddy has got to be mistaken! I just met that kid and still I can tell you he would not do that shit. That can't be!"

Dain said, "Yeah, she's badly hurt but recovering. I'm just as shocked as you are. And, yes, about his large family you spoke of. Jr. and his family are all well-known to everyone. They're whack-jobs."

"What? I cannot believe this! He and his family all seemed so nice and decent. They all helped me, and even prayed and talked about God and stuff. I just don't believe any of this."

"God, huh? That's funny. Listen, there's some really screwed up people in this world, and I'm sorry to have even told you this. I felt you needed to know about your friend Jr. He's crazy. I'd stay away."

I couldn't explain what I felt in that moment. I was confused. I had to find out from Jr. "I appreciate you telling me. I have got to get back to Tiana and be with my little girl. Thanks again, Dain."

I left Dain's and called Tiana and told her I was okay. I told her I was on the way home, and to head there now. I was excited to see Tiana and missed Taylor so much. As I got closer to our house, I noticed there were people in my front yard. *What the hell?* Some man was viciously kicking the shit out of another man and a woman, right in front of Tiana and Taylor!

"Hey, you fucker!" I yelled as I hopped out of my car and bolted to the aid of the young man and woman. They were lying on the ground, trying to defend themselves against the heavy onslaught. As hard as I could I jumped on top of the man, knocking him over. I got on top of him and the second I was about to drop down blows I realized that this man was Jr.!

"Max? What the hell are you doing?" I yelled.

Jr. looked at me, shaking his head. I looked over at the poor young woman and man on the ground, seeing they were beaten up as they writhed and moaned in pain.

"Help us! He's trying to kill us! He's trying to get them!" yelled the bloodied woman.

I looked over at my front porch, where Tiana and Taylor were standing, frightened and crying.

I looked back to Jr. with disgust and utter rage as I yelled, "You crazy, sick fuck! How could you?" I unloaded on Jr., hitting him repeatedly in his face, head, and neck. "Wha...wait! No..." Jr. said while trying to block the oncoming blows. With many hits getting through, Jr. bled from his mouth and nose. I got up off of Jr. and said, "You get the fuck out of here now! I heard what you did. Rapist! I know about you and your sick family!"

Jr. got up and hobbled backward.

"I believed you! I trusted you! I wished I would have killed you that day! I hate you! Now get the fuck out of here before I do kill you. I never want to see your face again. Stay away from me and my family!" I yelled.

Jr. replied with a cracked voice, "Caleb, please, I'm so sorry; it's not what you think. Don't believe that guy, Dain is..."

I cut Jr. off while I pointed my finger in his face and yelled, "Fuck you! Leave!"

Jr. lowered his head, turned around, and walked away.

All I could think about was how much of a sick and twisted pile of shit that guy Jr. really was as I watched him walk away. I turned back to the other two and saw they were severely banged up. I walked over to them, and when I did, I thought I recognized them. It looked like Joxel and Zitaya, Dain's brother and sister.

They must have been looking for me and tried to stop Jr. They were helping my family!

I went to help them, but for some reason they ignored me and hobbled down the street. They climbed into a car and drove away.

I turned to Tiana and Taylor and noticed they were no longer on the front patio. I ran inside to see if they were okay.

"No!" I yelled when I saw Tiana on the phone, assuming she was calling the police. I took the cellphone out of her hands and hung up. "Tiana, don't call the police, don't call anyone!"

"Caleb! What is going on, for the last time? Taylor is scared," Tiana yelled. As she tried to rock and comfort Taylor, I sat down and held them both. Later that night, I told her of all the bizarre things that had happened the last few days. I told her everything.

Tiana and I talked for nearly two hours as I explained it all. I confirmed her suspicions and confessed all the lies and secrets, and told her about my double life. I told her about my affair, my gambling debts, and money troubles, which all led to talking to Jimbo. And finally, I told her of my desperate act, the failed bank heist, trying to get it all back. And I also told Tiana I tried to kill myself.

Tiana, hysterical, covered her face and cried.

I told her how sorry and ashamed I was. I told her I hated myself.

I knew I could not tell Tiana everything right then. Not yet. I told her how I almost ran into Jr., met his large family, and had become close to them. She again asked about that guy she saw, Dain, who saved her and Taylor.

I told her how he was like no one I had ever met before. And, as crazy as it was, he said I owed him nothing for the large ransom. Although grateful, she suggested something seemed off about that. I told her that was how I felt and it turned out, Dain was legit.

I told her, ironically, they both had large families I had met. In spite of also wanting to tell Tiana of the two-wild night's at Dain's, I couldn't. The guilt and shame of what I had done were too much.

Tiana was shocked with disbelief, hearing all of this, as she continued to cry with her head down. She struggled to catch her breath. I reached for her, held her in my arms, and said, "I messed up bad. I made mistakes. I've always wanted to love you the right way. How I was and what I've done was not me. I want to get counseling and do whatever it takes for us and Taylor. I need you and Taylor in my life. I want my family back. Please forgive me. I love you." I had tears in my eyes.

At that moment, Tiana looked into my eyes and faintly said, "I don't care about the money, I don't care about what has happened or our problems. All I care about is you and our daughter. Yes, Caleb, all I wanted was to love you, too. I love you…" She held me tight, and we cried. I could not believe my ears, and I was elated, as my heart filled with joy. To hear those words from her was everything to me.

I held her close and my tears of regret and shame turned to happiness. I encouraged her to be strong as I still had to smooth a few things out. Her understanding made everything so much easier. I told Tiana this and said the dream I had of that young boy had to mean something.

And then it hit me! I recalled what Dain had told me when I was at his house. He told me the next time I saw Tiana, everything would change for the better. I couldn't believe it, and had to tell Tiana.

"Tiana! There is something else I have to share with you. Dain, that guy who helped me and saved you from Jim, also told me something this morning I disregarded." I stood with excitement and continued, "After talking to him of our problems, Dain said he wanted to help me and our family. In fact, he said the next time I talked to you, it would all work out for us." Tiana looked at me with a smile while I continued, "I never thought I would hear this from you, or even get another chance.

"Ever since I met Dain, everything has been so great and has worked out, and now this!" I added.

I had to tell Dain. I had to thank him for all he had done, for saving my family and so much more. I hugged and kissed Tiana and Taylor and told Tiana I had to go thank Dain and clear a few things up. I would be back. "Don't tell anyone you saw me until I come back. I have so much more to share with you. I love you," I said as I headed out to Dain's house, to thank him.

# 21

## WELCOME BACK

THAT EVENING, I pulled up to Dain's house and was greeted with a warm welcome. "Caleb! How's it going? Welcome back," Dain said. I was so excited I couldn't hold it in a second more. I said, "You're not going to believe this. Remember what you told me before I left home? Well, we talked and all I can say is, how the hell did you know?"

Dain replied with a grin. "You mean about you and your wife?"

"Yes! I told her everything, and somehow, she forgave me, and now we're going to reconcile. As I was talking to her, I remembered what you told me. You said the next time we talked it would all work out. How?"

"Man, that's so great to hear, and I'm happy for you. It only worked out that way because you believed and trusted me, and you started to believe what I said." He winked.

I said, "I'm so thankful for you. I don't know how you

continue to amaze and surprise me like this. Thank you, I owe you everything."

"It's my pleasure. Glad I'm able to continue to help you. That strong pull you have felt here and with me is for a reason. I think it's time you met someone. He can show you things you have never seen or heard before. He has taught me and enlightened me so much. How you're feeling now is just the beginning."

"Really? Sure, that would be cool, man. Also, there's something I wondered. Why were your brother and sister at my house? When I pulled up, I saw someone fighting brutally against who I thought was your brother and sister, Joxel and Zitaya. That one man beat the shit out of your brother and sister. As I intervened and stopped the man, I quickly discovered that the man was, Jr. Are they okay? Was that them?"

"Yes, that motherfucker! I just found out." He pounded his fist on the table.

Stadiel said, "Yeah, they called and they're getting treated in the hospital. They're not doing good."

"Well, now you know what I said holds true about your friend, Max Jr. I'm sorry you and your family had to see that. Are you okay?" Dain asked me.

I replied, "Yes, thanks. I was shocked. I didn't hesitate a second as I jumped on him, knocking him off of your sister, and started pounding him. I told Jr. to leave and never return as he eventually left".

I told Dain it was Jr. that tried to tell me to watch out for him. Then I recalled something.

"What you told me the other day at the club. What was that about? You said you're a hitman and you're going to kill me. Why?"

Dain laughed. He said, "I was drunk. Again, pardon my dry humor. I'm so sorry, again. Jr. is a lunatic and he will be taken care of."

"You mean you're calling the cops on him?"

Dain replied with a smirk, "Oh, no...we don't dial 911 here. We have our own ways of dealing with these kinds of matters."

"I see. Well, thanks for your help. You saved me and my family. I owe you big time."

"I got to ask, why is it exactly that you're doing this for me?" I added.

Dain replied, "We just like helping decent people with their problems. We all like you, and you fit in with us. This is one of the main reasons that bothered me to see a good person, like you with that nut. I'm glad you're okay and that I could help your hardships."

Dain made me feel at ease. His words were soothing and I felt good.

"A toast! To Caleb, who saved our brother and sister Joxel and Zitaya! And a special toast to his family as we welcome him to ours."

"Welcome back, man, our house is your house," Sorush said as the others cheered. "Here you go, Caleb," one of the sisters, Zariall said, giving me a drink. Dain once again mystified me with more of his magic as the others kicked off another wild night of partying and indulgence in every way. Knowing this was coming, I knew I would be ok with a few drinks and would shun anything more.

Thinking of Tiana, I looked at my cellphone and saw a flash notification that read, "Breaking news: Authorities say the perpetrator from the bank heist last Monday has been cornered and a gunfight erupted at a hotel on 24th Street. The sole bank robber made it clear he would not go without a fight, and was shot and killed by police officers. We later identified the man as James Thomas Barnes. It was also confirmed that he was the sole conspirator and there were no other suspects."

I continued reading the article: "Jim, a high executive at one of the top Fortune 500 banks in the world, Wayland Financial. Jim Barnes was believed to be involved in an inside stock trading scheme and was part of the notorious deadly Mirtaza family gang. Jim was linked to the robbing and murder of three people in cold blood two weeks ago, Wednesday."

My heart sank in disgust and relief.

*Oh shit! Wait, what did Dain say his last name was at the club that night?* I thought. I could not recall. I was so drunk. That's when I noticed it. Dain's arm!

As I looked closer at the big tattoo on Dain's arm and when I did, I was horrified as it read "MIRTAZA." Dain quickly covered his arm when he noticed I'd read his tattoo. My face was as if I had just seen a ghost. Dain asked with a smirk, "Is something wrong, Caleb?". I was speechless as everyone around me continued to party. The laughter seemed to be directed toward me.

Suddenly, I felt woozy, and lost my balance.

Everything came to a halt.

*Oh fuck! My drink, they spiked it,* I thought.

I felt lightheaded. I gathered myself. Suddenly, I felt bold. Like I didn't give a shit. I replied, "Oh, nothing. I was just admiring your tattoos, especially that one on your arm."

The party and music stopped as Dain grinned and replied, "You've heard of us, I take it?"

I replied, "Oh yes, I sure have."

"I see. Well, Caleb, this doesn't have to change anything. I'm not sure exactly what you have heard, however, you should never believe or trust everything on the internet, and especially the media," replied Dain.

Everyone stated laughing. Everyone around me was in slow motion.

They laughed sarcastically, looking at me while pointing. I didn't like any of this. I closed my eyes for a moment, unsure of what to do or how to handle this.

I thought, *Now, it made sense how Dain saved Tiana and Taylor from Jim. They knew each other!* I knew I had to play it off here. I had to change gears.

I started to laugh uncontrollably and said, "Oh, that's too funny! Man, I know what you mean. I don't listen to that media bullshit. I'm messing with you. I don't know anything. I seem to have spilled my drink; can I have another?" Dain and all the others laughed as they poured me another drink. I laughed and pretended to drink it, while purposely spilling it. It was all cool as the party carried on.

The next morning, I awoke from another wild night with a headache. I found myself in a bed in one of the rooms. I ran to the window, and saw I was still at Dain's. I was in one of the rooms upstairs, on the third floor. I walked out to the hallway. There was no one around, and it was eerily quiet as I wandered the hall and the rooms of the upstairs.

"Hello?" I yelled. There was no response.

I continued to explore the creepy hallways and rooms with bizarre paintings, statues, and furniture. Strange writings were visible all throughout the house in another language.

"Ah!" I heard.

The cry of what sounded like a young girl, down the hallway. I followed the noise and cries to a room and slowly cracked open the door. What I saw I could not have been prepared for.

To my horror, I saw a bloodied, nearly naked little girl with a gag in her mouth, lying on a cement table.

*Help the girl!* I thought. *No, there may be others in the room with her. Go get help!*

I carefully closed the door and I made my way downstairs to the living room's front door. I opened the front door and heard, "Leaving already, without saying goodbye?"

It was Dain.

I replied, "Oh, damn it! You scared the shit out of me. I'm

sorry. I didn't want to wake anyone. Thanks again for everything. Things are back to great. Again, thanks. Time to head home and get back to the normal grind. I'll be in touch, friend."

Dain smiled and replied, "Oh, of course. No worries, I understand. Yes, that would be good. When you do come back, as I said, there is something very neat and important I want to show you. It's time you meet that person I was telling you about. I know you're ready."

"Yes, for sure, that sounds good."

I shook Dain's hand and walked out.

# 22
# BLOOD TOKEN

I WAS DISTRAUGHT and horrified at the sight of that poor, bloodied, little girl. I could not get her out of my mind. *Those sick fucks!* After second thought, I couldn't just leave her like that.

*At least try to save her!* I thought. I got in my car, pulled down the road, and pulled over behind a bush.

I hurried back to Dain's house, out of sight, to the back. I hopped over a wall and sneaked inside the back gate. It was another bright, hot day, making me an easy target to spot if I wasn't careful. My adrenaline kicked in. I knew to be caught would be it. The coast seemed clear, and I wasted no time. I climbed the side of the house to the third floor.

I peeked through the windows of the rooms for the little girl, and saw nothing. *Where the hell did she go?* I wondered. With only a few rooms left, I carefully climbed to the next room's tinted window and looked in. I heard voices and looked closer, and to my horror, it was her. I saw the little girl, covered with blood, on a table. Dain and the others were standing around her, performing some kind of ritual.

*Damn monsters!* I thought. I tried to listen to what was being said, and realized they were not speaking English. It was that other creepy language I heard them speaking prior. I could not believe what I was looking at, as my heart began to beat through my chest. They were all dressed in unusual black and grey robes, and wore masks of different animals and stood in a circle.

I saw Dain's brother Joxel walk toward the window, right at me. *He saw me!* I thought.

I lowered my head out of view. I waited a few moments to hear something, and it was silent.

I carefully peeked into the window again and—"Oh fuck!" I said. I was staring right into the face of Joxel, who had all-black eyes with white pupils! Thrown back, I slipped and lost my footing, falling down to the roof below, making a thud. "Uh…oh, shit!" I uttered while grabbing my ankle in agony. It was sprained. Knowing my cover was blown in every way, I got up and slid down the side wall to the ground in pain. I hobbled out of the back yard and down a little ways, and hid inside a big bush. I could see them all rush out the back door, looking all over, and up on the roof for me.

I knew two things: one, how much my ankle was killing me, and two, I'd been spotted and if caught, I would not make it out alive. I waited as they looked for me. They finally headed back inside, and I didn't hesitate. I limped as fast as I could to my car. Quickly I started the car and got the hell out of there. I was relieved as I headed toward the main road, leaving a cloud of dust behind me.

When I grabbed my cell to call the police, I saw something. *What the?* I thought as I noticed a car coming up fast behind me. "Oh shit! Oh no! It's them!" I said. It was a car full of the Mirtazas.

I stepped on it, dodging and weaving through the winding

dirt road, trying to lose them as they kept up right behind me. If I could just make it to the main road I could shake them. I hit the main road and accelerated to ninety, 110, and up to 120, passing other cars as if they were standing still. "You kidding me? Shit!" I yelled when I saw the car chasing me was still not far behind.

I looked down and noticed my gas gauge was nearly empty.

*Just make it to a crowded area, and I will be okay,* I thought. And then I heard my back-driver's side tire go flat and lost control of the car.

I slowed as pieces of my tire began to shred apart, flying everywhere. Sparks shot from the now tireless rim as I noticed they were right on top of me, now. I had no choice, I had to pull over.

I pulled over to an abandoned gas station with not a soul in sight, other than a few passing cars. I tried to flag down anyone for help, but the cars continued down the road. I put the car in park, and there I sat as I watched the car full of people pull up behind me.

There was nothing I could do. I looked in my mirror and saw Joxel and Zitaya get out of black SUV and walked up to my car door. "Caleb, why are you running from us? What the hell is wrong with you?" Zitaya asked. "Dain has something else very important to tell you about that guy Jr., and it's not good. Jr. found out you were talking and stuff, and now Jr. is trying to kill you. He's fucking nuts!"

I couldn't believe my ears. Joxel said, "We tried to catch you before you left, and thought something was wrong when you took off like that. Were glad you're safe. C'mon, hop in. Let's head back so Dain can fill you in. We will come back after for your car and then escort you home to your family."

You know that certain look people give when they spout out nothing but pure bullshit? Yeah, it's that exact look Joxel gave me then. They know I was eavesdropping, back there. They knew what I saw.

But what choice did I have? They wouldn't let me just walk away. I had to wait for a better spot to get out.

"I see. No, I'm okay, sorry about that. I was just a little scared. I didn't recognize you guys."

Zitaya opened my car door and motioned me to the other car.

With a very uneasy feeling, I stepped out of the car. Joxel said, "Yeah you've been on edge the last few days. It's all cool, though. You had been through a lot. Just take it easy. I'm just glad you're okay." He put his arm around my shoulders and led me to the other car. I looked at Zitaya and back at Joxel, and at the others in the car. All of them had this awkward smirk on their faces. I opened the passenger door to the SUV where Dain's other broth-ers, Stadiel, Gibborim, and Rahmiel were sitting.

Out of nowhere, I heard a tire screech. I looked up and saw some other car pull right in front and block us in. The others were startled as Joxel said, "What the fuck? Who the hell?"

There we all sat, frozen for a few moments, staring at this mysterious car in front of us, unable to see through the dark tint. Suddenly the driver side door opened and someone calmly stepped out.

*Is that…? It is. It's Jr.!* I thought, frightened. Jr. slowly walked up to the front of the car with a sarcastic grin and casually said, "Why, hello there. I seem to have lost my way. Can any of you guys help me?" The others stared at Jr. with pale faces. Paralyzed, they looked at one another, perplexed. Within a matter of seconds, the countenance on Jr.'s face changed dramatically as he glared hard into the eyes of the others. I looked at Joxel, Zitaya, and the others, and they all had blank looks, as if they had just seen a ghost.

Jr. said, "I believe you all have something of mine," with a smirk. "Caleb, get in the car! Hurry!" Zitaya demanded. I proceed to get in the SUV as Jr. yelled, "Caleb, Stop! Listen to me! It's time you know what's going on and who you really are! You have to know what your truly capable of. I will explain all of this.

Listen inside and trust me. These guys you're with are not what you think!"

*What? This guy is unbelievable!*

Joxel yelled, "Oh, fuck you! Can you believe this crazy bitch? Too late, Jr. Caleb and all of us know of you. Caleb, don't listen to that piece of shit! Hurry, get in the car!"

Scared, I stood there like a statue. "Stadiel, take Caleb back. We will take care of him," Joxel said as the others got out of the car.

I heard Gibborim tell Joxel, "Are you crazy? He's a Mestre de Batalha... you know we can't take him, Jox. We need help"

*What? They can't take him? Mestre de Batalha?* I looked over at Jr., who stood alone before us with a confident glare, as he stared down the other five. I felt my heart skip a few beats, knowing this is about to take a turn for the worst any second.

Stad pushed me back toward the SUV, forcing me inside. Gibb, Rahm, Joxel, and Zitaya leaned inside the SUV and pulled out weapons: bats, knives, and chains. The four brandished them at Jr., speaking another language. There they stood, a few feet away, before the weaponless Jr.

Blood began to pour from my nose as fear consumed me. I watched helplessly frozen as Jr. said calmly, "Okay, Caleb, my brother. The fear you feel is not real. You must search within who you really are. It will all come back. Hang tight a moment. This won't take long."

It went tense. Like a standoff at the OK Corral, except this corral was hell. Jr. Faced the four of them while Stadiel rushed me into the SUV.

"Wait, no!" someone yelled. That's when it happened so fast that it was hard to comprehend. Jr. leapt across to the other four, landing on top of them as he hit them all at once. The hard hits could be heard a mile away as Gibb, Rahm, Zitaya, and Joxel swung bats, knives, and chains, hitting Jr. all over.

*Oh shit! They're going to kill Jr.! No!*

"Caleb! You know you can destroy these guys, easily! They are your real enemy! I don't need your help with these fucks here. But for the fun of it, knock their asses out! Do it!" yelled Jr.

"Just get in the car, Caleb! We have no time! Don't listen to that liar. He will kill you!" Stadiel demanded, as he tried to force me into the SUV.

I heard a shriek of pain. When I looked back up, Jr. said, "Damn it! Okay, Caleb, next one you can join in. Be with you in a moment."

Suddenly, Jr. went ballistic. He was kicking the shit out of them all with devastating blows. I had never seen such an effective fighting style before as Max Jr. displayed. He pounded them with such brute force, blood gushed everywhere. He used precise strikes combined with an acrobatic flow. He dismantled their own weapons and used them on them.

I could hear the cringing sounds of arms and legs being broken and faces being smashed as bodies were thrown to and fro. Moans of hurt and agony was heard.

It was like watching a ruthless gladiator fight an enemy with no armor or weapon, to the death.

Zitaya was the only one left moving as the other three laid motionless on the ground with Stadiel and I at the SUV.

In a faint voice, Zitaya said, "Take him back...Stadiel!"

Calmly, Jr. walked over to Zitaya and landed a crushing elbow to her face. The four were left in a bloody massacre of a mess. Jr. Casually walked toward us.

"Oh fuck! Fuck! Get in the damn car, Caleb! Hurry!" Stadiel yelled.

It didn't feel right and I resisted his attempts as he tried to shove me inside.

"Fuck this shit!" said Stadiel.

He let me go and got into their SUV. He drove away.

# 23

# HUNTED & THE HUNTER

THERE I WAS, looking at Jr., who had just taken out four people like a man possessed. He had to have killed them. Jr. was bloodied and panting with exhaustion. He looked at me as he held out his blood covered hands to me in a calm, peaceful gesture. He said, "Don't worry. I'm not going to hurt you. We have to talk, Caleb. Now is your time to know this truth."

I was scared shitless.

A burst of anger hit me, and I yelled, "Steroid-raged psycho! Are you on PCP or something? What do you want with me already? Who the hell are you? This is a secret government thing, isn't it? Joke's on you, buddy, because you're not getting my vote, or money. I'm flat-ass broke, and I don't believe in political puppet shows, not even as a kid. Go to the next person!"

"Also, I don't do business with murderers. You just killed these people in cold blood. Stay the hell away from me!" I yelled.

Jr. replied, "I know you're frightened and confused. But listen to me! This is what you have asked for. You're not who you think you are. You're way more. I'm here to remind you of who you really are and your purpose here. I'm telling you, if only you knew the power and gift you possess, and what you're capable of."

"Oh yeah?" I laughed.

"Yes. The reason you have always struggled is, this is not your home. Since your birth, you have been corrupted and pro-grammed with a deceptor over your eyes, a scale-like blinder. While they're on you won't be able to understand or see this."

Jr. added, "Your father, Caleb. The hurt and anger. Your burn-ing question of life and your purpose. Odd encounters, and a heavyset woman in an orange-red dress. You think that's all cir-cumstantial? Come on already, man. This is not that hard. You're beating yourself up, here. Actually, that's exactly what you need to do, beat your ass."

*What did he say? How could this guy know all of this?* I won-dered. No, he's not a psychic. Someone had to have told him and put him up to this.

"Shut the hell up, already. You don't really expect me to believe this shit, do you? I have no clue how you knew all of that about me; maybe you got it out of my mother or someone. Either way, I'm done here. I don't have time for any of this. I'm not going to be mind-fucked another second. If you don't get the hell away, I'm going to call the police."

"Caleb?"

"Yeah, what?"

"Can we please take a time out on this damn acting thing already for a second? Don't make this hard on me, no more role playing. I'm getting a headache. You know I hate this."

"What? You're insane!" I yelled.

Jr. said, "Damn it! Okay, listen, all of what I said is true. Now, I'm going to cut right to it. As I told you before, we know each other well and you are a badass. You have been sent here on a mission, Caleb, and you're failing it miserably. This is unlike you. Now, I have been sent here to bail you out."

"At first, a young, determined recruit was assigned to you. However, because of your high status, you have been made a huge target. The risk and danger were too great for an inexperienced guardian, and he has struggled ever since. And so, I was assigned to take over. The young recruit disagreed and did not accept that. He refused to give up on completing his assignment for you," said Jr. He held his head low as if remorseful.

"Ah, I see. So, you're telling me that you're my new guardian? I get it. Well, okay, thanks!" I turned to walk away and heard a moan come from one of the four on the ground. I saw Joxel trying to get back up. Jr. looked into his eyes, and he immediately fell back down.

Jr. opened his door. He said, "Hop in. We need to hurry. They will come back, looking for these four piles of shit. We have a lot to talk about your other friends there."

With a dead cell, no car, and confused as hell, I didn't hesitate. I got in the car and we drove off.

"Where are we headed?" I asked Jr.

"Back to my house. We need to regroup and inform my father what has happened. Dain is going to be pissed when he finds out what I've done to his family of rot."

Jr. added, "Yes, that person I thought I saw the other night at that club, BabeLand's, was Dain. I'm sorry, I failed back there. I got drunk and distracted and fell for that damn siren he sent over. Shit! I have been sick to my stomach ever since. If only I would have known it was Dain for sure."

"What? This is so crazy! Did you...?"

Jr. Replied, "What? Sleep with her? I said I messed up."

"No, damn it! I don't care if you been with her. Dain said you beat the shit out of her and raped her," I said.

"No. Caleb, that's not even close to the truth. I did not rape her. To say Dain is a master manipulating psychotic killer would be an understatement. I know him very well. And yes, he knows me. We have fought before and he beat me. Dain is the reason I'm taking over from your original young protector."

Jr. added, "The last encounter I had with Dain was a long time ago, at the much-anticipated elite sacred battle grounds in front of high elites from both sides. I had just been granted the coveted and rare status of Mestre de Batalha, which means, where I'm from here in Portugal, Battle Master. There we stood, face to face, two Mestre de Batalhas from both sides, as all the other high elites watched on. We fought for a good while. Although I put up a good fight, I lost. I was humiliated, mocked, and left ashamed."

*Sacred battle grounds? Mestre de Batalha?* Even though I knew this was all horseshit, I had to be careful not to set him off. He was more delusional than I thought. And he was a killer.

"Now, Dain is also assigned to you. I regret to say it; this is the reason why I haven't been there for you like I should have been. Now you know my history with Dain. But there is something else about him. Something I cannot tell you yet. I need to talk to my father first and how to handle this. We're at war," Jr. Said.

"War? Okay, guardian of mine, I forgive you. Listen, cool story and all, but hold that thought. I'm going to check on my family, and I have to piss. Pull over at that next stop."

I called Tiana, to check on her and Taylor, as we headed down the road to the next gas station. She and Taylor were fine. I couldn't believe what she told me next. She said Nalla had hopped the fence and run away sometime today. They searched for her and she was gone.

I was beside myself. I told Tiana hopefully Nalla would return soon and not to worry. I would see her later.

Jr. could see I was deeply saddened.

"Ah, man. I'm sorry to hear that. Don't worry, God's with her," Jr. said.

"I appreciate that. However, God has nothing to do with this."

We got to my side of town. We pulled into the gas station and I headed to the restroom as Jr. waited in the car. When I came back out to the car, Jr. said, "Now I have to go. Wait here, I may be a bit. I'll be right back."

He headed inside and I noticed a large brown dog hobble right in front of the car toward the store. The poor dog was scooting through the parking lot with only his front legs, and it appeared he'd gotten hit.

*Poor dog. Damn, he looks bad,* I thought.

I noticed the dog stop and sit there, looking around helplessly.

I saw a man start to back his truck up toward the dog, who couldn't move.

"Hey, stop! You're going to run over that dog!" I yelled. I got out of the car, holding both hands up, running in front of the badly hurt dog. The truck stopped in its tracks instantly and the young driver got out.

"Oh shit! Did I hit him?" the young man wearing large sunglasses asked.

"No, you didn't. I don't know where he came from or what happened to him. He came out of nowhere. It seems like his back legs are broken."

"Oh, damn! Let's move him out of danger of other cars, at least."

I helped the man move the whimpering dog around the side of the building.

I heard a crash in front of the store. I looked and the whole front window was shattered. *What the?* I heard scuffling inside. I looked inside the store and I saw a big black dog. *Nalla? There she is! I know it's her! She's fighting viciously with another dog and a man.*

Nalla was lunging of walls, viciously whipping her tail and

swinging her paws, skillfully fighting them both. *No way! I have never seen a dog fight like that.* She was beating their asses! *Where the hell is Jr.?* He must still be in the bathroom. Immediately, I ran to Nalla and yelled for Jr.

I was tripped.

I looked back and the hair on my neck stood up. The hurt dog was now standing on all fours, staring right at me and growling ferociously while foaming at the mouth through its sharp teeth.

The dog shook his body and revealed his true fur color. There was no mistaking who this dog was with that unique all white body and black head. It was Vex, with all-black eyes!

The young man with the truck looked at me with an evil grin and chuckled. He removed his shades and I saw it was Sorush, Dain's brother. I realized the dogs were Vex and Rue, and it was the other brother, Jyrel, who was inside with Rue fighting.

Sorush and Vex slowly walked toward me as I got up and stepped back. I was frightened.

I looked back and see their right behind me. "Jr.!" I yelled. Before I could process anything, Vex lunged at me so fast and hard it knocked me to the ground and knocked the wind out of me.

Nearly knocked out, I looked up. Sorush injected me with a syringe. He picked me up and put me in his truck.

Instantly I became weak and immobile as Sorush locked me inside the truck. Sorush and Vex rushed inside the store.

"Nalla!" I yelled.

Within a few minutes, all four of them came out, with no sign of Nalla or Jr.

My vision blurred.

They hopped in the truck and we drove away, as I lost consciousness.

# 24
## MY BOY

"HEY, BRO. WAKE up," I heard someone say. I opened my eyes and saw Dain standing over me. I was lying on a couch in what looked like a study with only Dain.

"Where am I?" I asked.

"You're at my house. Are you okay?"

"I feel like shit. How did I get here? I can't seem to remember anything…"

Dain replied, "It's a long story. We saved you, that's the important thing."

I sat up and looked around, trying to gather my thoughts. I couldn't recall anything. My mind was a complete blank. "I'm glad you came back to us, you're safe here."

"I came back? What am I safe from?"

Dain responded, "Yes. Jr. kidnapped you and I sent help to save you. You're safe now from him and his psychotic family. As I said, they're trying to destroy your life."

Even with my mind clouded, I knew what he said did not sound right.

"I didn't want to have to tell you this, Caleb. There's just no other way around it, now. Not only has Max Jr. been trying to kill you, he has also been pursuing your wife this whole time."

"What? What did you say?"

"Yeah, I'm sorry. You recall that day you went home and he was already at your house in the front yard, fighting? Well, he was with your wife, trying to seduce her. How do I know this, you're thinking? After hearing some of your marital issues and problems the other day made me think."

Dain added, "Seeing the stress on your face made me very concerned. I wanted you to come back and help you. So that's when I sent Joxel and Zitaya to your house, and that's when they saw Jr. there with your wife and confirmed it. Oh, that look on your poor little girl's face. She was so confused and upset."

My mind cleared instantly when I heard that. There was no more confusion, I added it all up. Dain's underlined cold heart and cutthroat demeanor. His freak family behavior and disturb-ing parties. And that poor innocent little girl covered in blood. They attacked me and Nalla at the gas station. Now he said that? Nah. This is not me. I want no part of this.

*Jr. may be crazy, but this guy is one demented sicko. I'll stick with my gut here. Liar.*

*It's my turn to mind-fuck.*

I yelled, "You're fucking kidding me! That piece of shit...I will kill him!"

Dain said, "Don't worry; he will be taken care of. Listen, I know you may have heard a few things about us, here. One of that being we're the Mirtaza family. We are. As I told you, what you have heard about us is not true just as I said. We have been seriously misunderstood for a long time."

"We have powerful and serious influences, which help us help others. And this is something you can be a part of. I see your potential so much it's scary," added Dain.

"Oh, I know. I feel good here. You and your family have embraced me from the start. Most of all, you have saved my family. How would I be a part of what you're saying?"

"Yes. That's the other reason we wanted you back. I want to bring you in with us, Caleb. You're ready and you will be a huge asset for us. Your mind is about to be blown. I want you to meet the one who leads us, Lucio."

I said, "Lucio?

Dain replied, "Yes. He is the one who has helped me open my mind to everything. You will be fully enlightened and uplifted. Once you join us, your financial woes and worries will be over. In order for us to help you fully, though, you have to join us."

Enlightened? My troubles and finances would be taken care of? At the cost of another blood sacrifice? *Fuck that! This psychotic murderer!* I can only act so much. I'm done with this freak secret society bullshit. No money or reward can buy me for this.

I told Dain I would think about it. It was getting late and I had to get back home. Dain, however, insisted I at least check it out. He wanted me to meet Lucio.

My stomach sank when I noticed that look. I knew he would not let me leave.

Suddenly, I felt something. I realized I didn't have to be scared. I keep choosing to be. And, I've always known this. I know I can outsmart him. I can outdo him. Yet, as much as I knew this, there was something stopping me. I feel like a bomb ready to explode on him. For some reason I couldn't do it!

This entire time I had been held back. *Why?* "I can see you're troubled. Something vexes you. I don't want you to feel pressured. Stay the night tonight and rest. Tomorrow you can see for yourself what I've been saying. You will be awakened when you meet Lucio. You won't regret it," Dain said.

Even though he made it seem I had a choice, I knew I didn't. I went along with it for now. Sleeping with these freaks was the last thing I wanted. *Man, I hate this prick.* In front of Dain, I called Tiana letting her know I would be home the next day and had to stay as part of repayment.

I, however, already knew that was not going to happen. Tonight, while they slept, I was getting the hell out of there.

That night, Dain showed me to a room. He told me he would see me in the morning and to rest. He closed the door. *This is not the room I slept in before,* I thought. I walked into the large room and immediately the scent of old must hit me. It smelled like decay. It was like an old church with stained-glass windows.

The room was somehow darkly dimmed red with no lamps. The eyes in the pictures, from the mid-century figures, were unsettling. It was as if they were real. I wanted to walk right back out. I knew I couldn't, not yet. I looked around the room and I became more disturbed.

The beast-shaped Victorian bed was hypnotizing, with strange markings. The crosses on the wall appeared to bend. The mirror was blackened and seemed to call to me. A familiar fear hit me and I sat in the animal-shaped chair to gather myself. I looked up and noticed the strange, black, red, and gold tapestries were made of a type of beige Hyde.

*What the hell?* I felt something move.

I looked down at the armrest and realized what it was. *Flesh! This fucking chair is alive!* The arms and legs of the chair grabbed me and I struggled to break free. I heard hissing. A lizard-like tongue wrapped around my neck and choked me. *I can't breathe!*

The small figures in the pictures turned into zombies and slowly crawled along the wall toward me. The angels in the stained-glass windows turned demonic, and flew toward me with outstretched hands.

That same wicked figure I saw in my bathroom emerged from the dark mirror and crawled toward me, backward.

I broke free, ran toward the door, and noticed the room was smoky. The vent on the floor had smoke seeping into the room.

Dizziness hit me. I reached for the doorknob and stumbled to the floor.

*Ahhh, I feel so groggy.* I awoke to the howls of the night outside. I was on a bed. I sat up on the side and realized I was still in the room. *I'm losing it!* The room was now darker. I looked at my watch, and it was 3:22 a.m. It was time to get the hell out. I stood and panned the room and felt my skin crawl. There, in the dark corner, was the silhouette of a figure. There was someone sitting in the chair. I was paralyzed.

"Dain?" I said faintly.

There was no response.

My breathing intensified through an unsettling silence. I knew I had to be strong.

He growled.

*Oh, fuck that!* I thought, and dashed toward the door and opened it. But, I did not go through it. Something triggered. *Listen within? I'm a badass?* The effect of Jr.'s words struck me to the core.

I turned and faced him through the darkness.

He stood. "Caleb ..." he said.

I recognized that voice. *It's not Dain's. It was him!* The many nights he would chase me and I would run. My tormentor of the night.

I felt my nose. There was no blood. I closed the door back and locked it. *I'm not running anymore. And, neither is he.*

I clinched my fists and heard my knuckles. *Fuck him, too!* I ran to hit him and noticed his head was down. He slowly looked up at me ... *What?* I thought in horror.

I was face-to-face with myself.

"Hello, Caleb. My boy…" he said with an evil chuckle.

With a wicked grin, he raised an eyebrow. Suddenly his eyes became large as he tilted his head back, and before I could blink he head-butted my nose, knocking me to the ground. "Uh…" I uttered as I sat up in shock. I looked at my hands and saw they were covered in blood. My vision began to blur and everything slowed.

He laughed as he stood over me. I turned over onto my hands and knees and saw the splatter of my gushing nose.

This is why my nose has bled. My reminder of him. It was at this moment my whole life hit me, and I was reminded of the person I had become.

My entire life, I've listened to the deceptions and lies that surrounded me. I believed what life is supposed to be about. My double life. My mother's desperate cries. My daughter, whom I muted and crippled forever. The echoing gunshots that killed my father, who sacrificed his life so I could do all of that? All of this because of me.

No. It was because of him!

He is the who has guided me. I believed and trusted him! And he turned me into someone else! This is my true enemy. A remnant of the person I once was now stands before me. This is not me. My fists felt hot and began to glow with rage. *Deceptor!*

"Well, what are you waiting for? You know what time it is. It's time to run," he said with a sarcastic chuckle.

My eyes began to water. I wiped them; it was blood. Without a word, I looked up and swung and hit that motherfucker in the face so hard I felt my fist crack his skull.

He struggled back to his feet. "Wow. I didn't think you had it in you. You, however, just fucked up. You will never defeat us!" Before he had a chance to gather himself, I charged. *Wham!* I pummeled him on the ground. I roared with a rage from deep within, and I unloaded fists, elbows, and knees on him. I hit him with everything I had, as hard as I could. Blood was everywhere.

His face was bludgeoned, as he spit out his teeth. He looked at me, unfazed, and laughed. Suddenly he caught my fists and fought back. I grabbed him and punched him in his throat.

I stood over him as he desperately gasped for air. I reached my hands around his neck, while he shook his head.

I looked into his fear-filled eyes as he grabbed my arms with his weakened hands. With no hesitation, I squeezed. "I'm not your boy." I continued squeezing until his last breath.

He gargled and gasped as his eyes slowly closed and he fell to the ground.

I killed him.

I stood over his now lifeless body, knowing he would plague me no more. I knew Dain would continue to pursue me and eventually put my family at risk. I would stay and confront Dain.

# 25

# KNOCK-KNOCK

I T WAS THE next morning, and I felt different. I felt surprisingly bold and fearless. *What the shit?* I looked around, and for a second I thought I was in another room. I wasn't. Everything in the room was different. The windows and mirrors were clear and not darkened. The chair and bed and the pictures were regular normal old antiques.

I looked back as I walked out and thought, *Fuck that room!* I shut the door.

I was ready to go along with meeting Dain's friend. After, I would decline his offer and leave. "Morning, Caleb. I trust you slept well," said Dain. "Like a baby," I replied.

"Follow me," said Dain, and we headed down the hallway

He led me upstairs, to a fourth-floor, dimly lit room filled with candles.

*What the? How did a fourth floor appear out of nowhere?* I thought.

"Where is this Lucio?" I asked.

Dain replied, "Oh, he's here. We have already been preparing for this. You have always been one of us."

*One of us?*

I walked into the middle of the large, dark room, filled with statues and bizarre markings. There I stood, surrounded by Dain's brothers and sisters—the notorious Mirtaza clan. All of them were wearing odd-looking red and black sleeveless robes, exposing their striking tattoos and body art. The art on their bodies was like nothing I'd seen before.

I proceeded with what appeared to be some sort of ceremonial ritual.

The lights dimmed as others behind me start chattering softly in an unknown language. The entire room that surrounded me began to change its look and color before my eyes.

Four others walked into the room, wearing white robes, as a light mist of smoke covered the floor. Dain's sisters, Amitiel and Zariall came out of the darkness topless. Mist seeped up from beneath my feet and shot into my nostrils. I was dizzy, in a trance-like state. Amitiel gave me a drug, putting it in my mouth as both sisters caressed, kissed, and fondled me.

"All there is to do, Caleb, to become enlightened and freed in every way, to become powerful, is to deny all other gods and swear a life oath and allegiance to our god, Lucio, the angel of light."

*Angel of light? Hell no!* I thought. *I want to get this shit over with and get the fuck out.*

The mist thickened and filled the dark room. Dain stood in front of me, raised his head and hands, and said, "To you, light-bearer Lucio, we give Caleb…"

I looked around and saw I was surrounded by others. They all continued to chant in an unknown tongue while waving their heads in a circular motion.

"Join us, Caleb… become one with us and live like a god," Zariall whispered and licked my neck.

*Bam!* I heard a bang as Dain and the others look at each other, confused. *Thud! Boom!* Louder and closer the banging continued. Dain pointed to a few of his brothers, to go investigate.

*I know exactly what that banging is. Jr.!*

The bangs and the thuds became even louder as the others in the room looked around, concerned, and looked at Dain.

Dain walked toward me with Ithuriel and Valoel, his other naked sisters and the four sisters kissed and rubbed me all over as they moaned.

Dain held his hand out in front of me as a mystical, beaming, white orb appeared in his hand.

I looked into the orb and saw myself. Inside the orb I saw that I had everything I ever wanted. People were bowing before me, and I was surrounded with lavish things of all kinds. It was as if I was having it now, as it all was so real.

I reach out to the inviting orb, and when I did, I heard within. I started to feel the new found strength and my fists felt hot.

I looked at Dain. "Fuck you and your god!"

Shocked, Dain's eyes grew large and he stumbled backward.

In a fit of rage, Dain yelled in a bizarre language and his face began to morph and distort into something or someone else.

Dain said, "Why Caleb, you disappoint me. After all I have done for you and your precious wife and daughter."

I heard someone else say in a low, demonic grumble, "Perhaps you just need to witness the sheer power we yield. Behold the power of the one and only true god...Lucio!" I realized, it was Dain.

He closed his eyes and slowly raised his arms, his palms up halfway, as Joxel, Gibborim, Rahmiel and Gadriel emerged from the dark and stood by his side.

Dain began to levitate and the lights and candles flickered, and it went pitch black.

His tattoos began to illuminate and glow with a beaming, light-blue color, revealing hidden messages exalting Lucio.

"All to the enlightened one. Glory and praise to god, the angel of light," I read on one of Dain's arms. The other arm read, "True god—Light Bearer."

The chants and utterings continued.

Dain opened his eyes, and when he did, they were all white.

I was surrounded by Dain's brothers and sisters, who also had white eyes as their tattoos began glowing. The faces of the four sisters standing around me morphed until they were inhuman. Their gentle touch turned to clawing and hisses.

"Jr., in here! Help me!" I yelled.

I heard moans of agony and pain from outside the bedroom door.

"The door!" yelled Joxel.

*Krrsshhh!*

The door to the room was smashed through. As the dust settled in the dimly lit room, a shadowy figure stood in the doorway.

Dain lowered to his feet. The lights came back on. Everything was normal again. I saw it was him, it was Jr.

He stepped forward into the dull lighting and was alone.

Humatiel, one of the brothers, uttered, "Mestre de Batalha," and stepped back.

Breathing heavily, and covered in blood, Jr. had the most intense look of sheer furry as he stared down Dain.

"Bitch," said Dain.

Jr. clinched his fists.

"Little Jr., I don't believe it was locked. So, I guess the jig is up, huh?" Dain said with a smirk.

"Jr.! Help, they're hurting me!"

With a shake of his head, Jr. looked at me, "Hurting you, really? C'mon already, Caleb, you don't need my help! It's like I have been telling you all along, you're one bad motherfucker.

Remember what you did last night? You have the ability to destroy everyone in here, alone."

*Last night? He knows?*

"And, what's hilarious, is all these other fucks around you already knows this. They don't want you to know or remember. I'm not the only bad actor here," chuckled Jr.

I felt a groaning inside.

"Fuck you," said Dain.

Dain stepped in front of us all and waved his hand to his brothers and sisters, motioning them to get behind him. Zitaya and Amitiel kept their grasp and dug their nails into me tighter.

There they were, Dain and Max Jr. standing face to face, staring each other down. The intensity of the room was thick. It went silent.

Dain laughed wickedly and his eyes rolled back. The lights flickered and he raised his palms upward and chanted. Jr. turned to me. He said, "Stay strong and listen to me. Right now, I'm the one who is going to need your help. I won't be able to do it alone this time. I need you to unleash that power within you. Now c'mon, Caleb, snap out of it! Let's fuck their world up. Just like old times," added Jr.

# 26

## TIT FOR TAT

HIS WORDS BEGAN to ring louder in my ears… I looked at Dain levitating before me. Jr. turned back to Dain and to my surprise, he spoke their strange language. Dain raised his arm and pointed in Jr.'s face.

Jr. yelled, "Trazem!" which I knew meant "Bring it" in Portuguese.

Without warning, one of Dain's brothers lunged right at Jr. from behind, grabbing him. Jr. threw him off as four others swarmed Max Jr. from all sides.

"Caleb! Get them!" yelled Jr.

*He needs my help!*

I looked down and my fists felt hotter and lit up.

I lunged to help Jr., and was stopped by Zataya and Valoel.

"Caleb!" Jr. yelled.

My veins. I felt something surging through them and glowed. I felt stronger.

*What's this? What's happening to me here?*

My anger fueled me.

A surge shot through me and I swung, hitting the two sisters next to me and they flew back. I was quickly knocked to the ground by the others. I struggled to break free. They bound me with ties and taped my mouth. All I could hear were grunts and thuds as bodies flew everywhere as Jr. fought them all. *Wham! Wham!* Over and over I heard the hits of vicious sounds of pounding of flesh. Jr. noticed I was in trouble.

Max Jr., the mad man, thwarted and dodged blow after blow, countering with flying kicks and brutal punches to the head and faces of his attackers while trying to reach and help me.

Through the busted-out bedroom door, three of the other hurt and bloodied brothers from downstairs hobbled in, carrying bats, knives, and chains to aid the others. Jr. was somehow able to absorb many blows. I looked at Dain and noticed he was not fighting, for some reason.

Blood gushed everywhere as Jr. dismantled his attackers. Jr. clenched his hands and double-hammer down, pounding all in his sight as fatigue began to set in. The sound of crushing blows and bones breaking was disturbing to hear. Jr., the madman, wrecked them all.

Suddenly the room went quiet.

Dain remained in a meditative trance. His tattoos began glowing and illuminating light-blue beams that lit up the dark room. Dain opened his eyes, which were now again solid white. Dain's sisters began chanting in an unknown language.

All I could hear was Jr.'s heavy panting from the many hard-fought battles.

In a faint voice, Jr. said, "Caleb, dammit! I need your help. I know you feel it too. You can do it. They can't stop you. Help…"

I saw Jr. fall to one knee, from his wounds and fatigue.

I kicked and turned and tried to break free. I couldn't.

Three of the sisters picked up their wounded brothers and

took them into the next room. Zitaya picked me up over her shoulder and followed. I watched Jr. on the way out. *My Dad...* It was if I relived it again. Sadness and anger were all I felt inside. They shut the door behind us.

Jr. was now in the room with Dain, alone.

*No! He can't fight anymore! He can't even stand!* I thought.

*Dain is going to kill him!*

There was a pause. Then I heard it. A shrieking roar and a loud thud. The sounds of vicious fighting echoed outside the door.

My heart sank.

The fighting in the other room stopped. Not a sound was heard as all eyes were fixed on the bedroom door. The doorknob turned a few times as the others look around with uncertainty.

The door opened. It was Dain.

Blood seeped in from the floor behind him. The room erupted in celebrations praising Dain.

Dain looked at me with a wicked grin. "Oh, Caleb. You broke my heart," said Dain.

They blindfolded me. *Whack!* I was hit on the head and knocked out cold.

# 27

# A SACRIFICE

*O*H, *MY HEAD,* I thought. *I can't see!*

Realizing I was still blindfolded, I was able to remove it. I stood up and I found myself in some kind of large graveled area.

A construction site?

"Well, hello, Caleb," a familiar voice said, behind me. I slowly turned around and to my horror, on a platform, stood Dain, Joxel, and Zitaya, with Tiana and Taylor kneeling in front, bound and tied.

"No!" I screamed and charged at them. Then I stopped in my tracks. On the ground ahead were the two vicious dogs, Vex and Rue. On leashes, they lunged and pulled toward me, held back by Sorush. "No! Take me! Leave them out of this! Please!" I yelled.

"Oh no. After all I have done for you. So ungrateful. You betrayed me. You have chosen wrong just like your dead friend did. I saved your precious family for you. Remember? And now I'm taking them back!" replied Dain.

Out from behind Dain, and below and out of the darkness, emerged the entire Mirtaza family gang. All of Dain's brothers and sisters stood before me.

Dain looked down with an evil. sarcastic smirk, with Tiana and Taylor bound on their knees in front of him. Tiana began to cry as she held her head low with closed eyes. My little girl looked at me, helplessly crying, unable to speak, as she struggled against her restraints.

I was completely helpless. I had never felt such anger as I ground my teeth and clenched my fists. I began to convulse, writhing in anger and agony.

I heard Vex and Rue, walk toward me, growling with saliva dripping from their sharp teeth. I shook my head in a daze as the dogs got closer. I looked at Tiana and Taylor, bound and frightened.

"Now a sacrifice," Dain said.

"Oh my God! No!" I yelled.

As he spoke, Tiana and Taylor began to rise, strapped to a crane lift. They rose over the edge of the half-built building with long straps. "For your betrayal and defiance, a sacrifice I'm going to make. Since, I'm now the rightful owner of Tiana and Taylor, I'm offering only one of them as a sacrifice to my god, Lucio. Which one shall I choose?"

I ran toward them and screamed, "No! You fuck! I said take me! Don't hurt them!"

I was stopped in my tracks by Vex and Rue. "Caleb, oh God!" Tiana cried out.

Dain laughed.

I replied, "No, I beg you, please!"

With an evil smirk, Dain waived his finger at me, while he shook his head. He looked up to where Tiana and Taylor dangled above, and reached behind his back and pulled out an axe. He threw it. It hit the strap holding Taylor, cutting it off.

"No!" I screamed, with an outstretched hand. All I could

do was watch in horror as Taylor fell seventy feet, behind a big dump truck.

I yelled again, helplessly, at the top of my lungs. Tiana screamed, crying hysterically. Everything began spinning around me. I fell to my knees.

I became lightheaded and everything was a blur. I tasted blood from my mouth from grinding my teeth. I knelt, motionless, staring at the ground.

"Caleb! No!" I heard.

I looked up and there was Dain, still holding Tiana by her hair. "Caleb! Taylor? No! Ah!" Tiana screamed. "Help her, Caleb! Oh, God!" she said.

I looked at Tiana, who was bound, crying uncontrollably.

# 28
# THE AWAKENING

HOW CAN ANY *god allow such things to happen?* Who was I kidding? There is no God. We were truly alone. I was not going to take it lying down another second.

I looked at Tiana one last time as she looked back and nodded. I could feel Tiana's heart. I knew we had nothing left. It was up to me. I knew what I had to do. I would fight.

I got up and I looked at Dain. With all my anger and rage I charged. I was quickly knocked down by Vex and Rue. They foamed at their mouths as they barked and snapped their jaws in my face. Sorush called them back and they returned to their master.

"Careful, there, Caleb. I failed to mention my dogs love to play fetch with flesh," said Dain, and chuckled.

From the half-built structure above where Dain stood, to the ground below, Dain's brothers and sisters jumped, climbed, and swung down and headed for me. Straight ahead, out of the shadows, emerged Joxel and Zitaya.

All I could do was watch as they all headed for me. From the other direction came Kasbiel, Stadiel, Gibborim, and Rahmiel, along with all the others, as they got closer and closer.

I began backpedaling. Suddenly they all charged right at me. "No!" Tiana screamed.

I backed up faster and backed into something behind me.

"What the fuck?" Dain's brother, Kasbiel, said.

I looked up and noticed all of Dain's brethren had stopped dead in their tracks. I turned around, and it was Max Jr., standing right behind me, bloodied with a look of rage in his eyes as he stared down all of Dain's brethren.

"Caleb! Look...Taylor!" Tiana screamed while pointing to the loader truck where little Taylor had fallen.

I looked and I couldn't believe it. It was my little girl! Taylor was sitting peacefully on top of the truck as she reached her arms out to me.

"This bitch fuck still?" Dain said.

"You really think this weak piece of shit is going to save you, Caleb? He's a pathetic joke!"

All I could see were thirteen or so psychopaths of the Mirtaza family gang in front of us. I was so scared for Tiana and Taylor; *they're going to kill them! I don't care about me;* I just couldn't take losing my wife or daughter again.

I looked at Max Jr., confused. He shook his head and said, "C'mon now already Caleb, don't look at me. You're the most powerful one here. I told you, you're one true badass. And, damn it, where were you at back there, huh? I think my arm is broke. Damn, I hate this prick Dain so bad."

Jr. added, "Caleb! Listen for the last time. Just shut your mind up and listen to what's filled inside of you. You can do this. You still have yet to complete your mission here and we have your family to save. Now stop the bullshit and fucking help me!"

"Damn, this is frustrating as hell. I'm going to need a drink after this before we head back home. This shit here sucks," added Jr.

*I have no damn powers! What the fuck?* I thought. I could not handle anymore. *Tiana and Taylor need help!* I needed something more. *I need help!*

I eased my mind and I listened to Jr.

For the first time, I released it all and I fully listened within.

"Mate ele!" Dain yelled, which I knew meant "Kill him!" in Portuguese.

I looked at Dain's family and they walked toward me and Max Jr.

From the depths of my heart and spirit, I uttered, "If you can hear me…I don't care about me. All I ask is to please save my little girl, and my wife. I'm so sorry. I feel what you have put inside me. I hear you. Please… I need you," I prayed.

A jolt surged through my body, jerking me back. I opened my eyes and fell to the ground in shock. I was in awe of what I was now looking at.

All that was before me a bit ago changed. It was as if I was in an entirely different place. Everything around me illuminated with bright white and yellow light. All of Dain's henchmen, even Vex and Rue, were bigger, and they glowed darkly.

They had eyes that beamed with red rays of light. They wore battle armor that was dark and sinister. They had large blue wings while others had white wings, with all having a trim of fire. Joxel's wings were blue with a trim of white fire. *What is all this? What's happening?* I wondered

Dain's now transformed mighty brethren were a lot bigger, in dark, enchanted, black battle armor. They displayed mighty weaponry, firing it into the air as they displayed great powers. Dain's brethren had shields of fire-breathing dragon heads. The dragon heads were actually alive on their shields!

Dain's dark brethren had slingshots that fired black scorpions of fire. Some of the dark brethren had enchanted staves of live serpents that fired smaller black, live fire serpents from their mouths.

Some brethren were casting black fire orbs. Others had surging lightning shields around them and fired bolts of lightening.

I was paralyzed at the sight as they wielded their enchanted weapons. I realized I could see everything in the far distance as if it were close. I looked over and saw little Taylor also looked different. Her body had a greyish blur about her, and yet I could still see her face plain as day as she continued to cry.

"Remember, Caleb, nothing beats a smile," a familiar sarcastic voice said from above.

I looked up and my jaw dropped. There stood the transformed Dain, with an evil smirk, looking down at me. Dain's dark armor was epic, compared to the others. His eyes beamed red flames and his striking armor was of black fire. His wings were red and transparent, with a black fiery trim that lined his wings as he held a sword of black flames.

I looked at Tiana and noticed she was trying to tell me something. I couldn't make it out. Dain grasped the chains that bound Tiana, along with her long hair, and jerked the chains hard. Dain pointed down at me as his brothers advanced towards us, and sent others to little Taylor. "No!" I screamed with outstretched hands. I dropped to my knees and felt completely helpless.

"Don't be afraid. We got you, Caleb, my brother," a calm voice said behind me.

*We?* I repeated to myself and looked up.

Dain's brothers were all standing there with looks of horror on their faces. I turned around slowly and I was baffled. It was, the now calm Maximino Jr. I heard. Jr. also looked completely different. He was glowing with pure radiance, and much larger, with beaming eyes of blue fire. His majestic armor was enchanted, with red and white flames. It was so stunning and brilliant; I could barely look.

His breathtaking red wings were also transparent, with black fiery trim. Standing behind Max Jr. stood six of his brothers and his sister: Michael, Kyra, Arron, Camden, Logan, and Jaden, who were all in glowing white and gold battle-hardened armor with eyes of beaming blue rays and radiant, blue wings with a trim of fire. Michael's blue wings had a trim of white fire.

*They really are angels!* I thought in excitement.

Max Jr.'s light angelic brethren had shields of roaring lion heads that were also alive, with eyes of beaming white light. And, just like their enemy counterparts, Max Jr. and his angelic siblings possessed great powers and weaponry.

Michael wielded a mighty sword of blue flame. I saw him teleport around us to different positions and ready for battle. Arron had an axe of black and blue fire. He conjured up water from a nearby water tank. He manipulated the water into small elemental warriors. Logan had a slingshot of white fire who displayed the ability to call upon the winds around us.

Camden had an electric cloud bow that fired electric cloud arrows, who could manipulate electricity from the nearby power lines. Kyra wielded a blue flaming boomerang that multiplied when thrown and reunited as one upon its return. She leapt into the air and morphed into a blue transparent battle eagle.

Jaden smashed the ground with both fists and shook it. He had the strength of a machine. He wielded an enchanted, white, flaming double-sided war hammer. They all glared and swayed back and forth and were ready for battle.

My legs became weak at the sight of them all. Like Jr.'s other brethren, they were all decked out in gleaming white and gold enchanted plating with glowing blue and other's white, wings trimmed with fire. They all stood in fighting stances, swaying back and forth with fierce, glowing weapons.

A tense standoff ensued.

"Morte ao traidor!" Dain yelled from on top of the construction building. Somehow, I knew it meant "Death to the traitor."

"Morte ao traidor!" the others chanted.

They have all spoken in Portuguese the whole time. *How the hell do I even know that?* I thought, confused.

"No, Dain. It is you that is the traitor. You betrayed us," Max Jr. replied, while he pounded his chest. "Trazem!" Max Jr. yelled, which I again knew meant, "Bring it!"

*Dain betrayed?* I wondered.

Max Jr. reached behind his back, grasping his two mighty swords. The second he grasped them, the swords ignited into bursting red swords of flame, with black flaming centers. There I stood in the midst of these giant angelic warriors. I was so terrified, I pissed myself.

I heard mighty roars overhead. I looked up to see Max Jr.'s brothers, Michael and Camden, charge over my head as Arron led the others. Dain's dark brethren roared as they dashed ahead, engaging them in battle. Beams of intense light and fire soared back and forth. Grunts of pain echoed loudly through the vicious clashes of the mighty weapons.

Standing in the midst of it all, in a battle stance, was Maximino Jr., who never left my side. "I'm ready when you are Caleb. Let me know when you're ready to attack," Jr. said. I looked at Jr., confused. I tried to comprehend what was happening around me.

High above, on the half-built structure, stood Dain, watching as the battle unfolded before him as he grasped Tiana's hair. Suddenly all the other angelics leapt up with great velocity, fiercely battling each other in midair. I was scared as hell.

The chaos and brutality overhead, was overwhelming. There was hacking and slashing of brute weaponry. Red blood splattered everywhere, from the golden angelic warriors, with each crushing blow. Black blood gushed from the dark angelics.

*How can they withstand such devastating blows?* I wondered.

Jr.'s family of light angelics were outnumbered, yet, they continued to fight relentlessly.

I turned to run but I couldn't move. My feet were literally

stuck to the ground. "Ah!" I yelled. "What's going on here? Jr. help me!"

"My brother, we don't run. We can't. We fight," said Jr.

His words pierced me and began to trigger something. I felt something stir inside.

I heard sounds of bone breaking and grunts of pain. Dain's dark brethren gained the upper hand. I felt antsy. There was a struggle with me and my breathing intensified.

It was disturbing to witness such chaos and brutality. Until it wasn't.

It hit me. I felt what Jr. had said. A flash back from my high school fighting days reminded me, I don't run. This all looked familiar. This carnage did not bother me. It fueled me. I loved it. My hands began to feel heavy and hot.

Michael, the elder of light angelics, surged with fierce rage, swiftly taking out three of the dark angelics. Camden and Logan vigorously fought the others as the light angelics gained control. Kyra swooped down from above and fired her talons, striking the enemy below. From above, Kyra guarded Arron who commanded his vicious water elemental's as they attacked.

Jaden dove into the ground like a drill and emerged up through the ground, plowing through the stumbling wounded enemy below, catching them off guard. I looked at the bloody massacre before me, and I realized the light angelics were winning.

Out of nowhere, Dain dashed through the air, plowing through Logan and Jaden, knocking them out. Dain dismantled the other light angelics, quickly regaining control of the battle.

"Ready now?" said Jr., and look down.

I looked down and my fists! They had a glow of blue fire around them.

"I'm ready," I replied.

Jr. nodded, and said, "That's my brother." His countenance changed to an intense, fierce look. He slowly turned toward Dain and pointed right at him. He leapt into the air and dashed on top of Dain, pummeling him to the ground. Dain charged right back and tackled Max Jr. as they viciously battled each other. *Whoosh!* I heard, as Maximino and Dain leapt up, fighting each other in the air.

"Tiana and Taylor!" I yelled. I saw Tiana alone, high above, on top of the half-built building, still bound in chains. I looked to my left and could see Taylor still on top of the big loader truck. I ran as fast as I could to my daughter. I couldn't believe how fast I ran. A burst of wind boosted me. I was immediately tackled by those two demon dogs, Vex and Rue.

They induced overwhelming fear on me. My nose gushed blood. All I saw were their long fangs. I yelled in horrific pain as they clamped down on my arms with their jaws and began dragging me away. While being dragged, I looked into their eyes and they whimpered. Suddenly, I remembered them well.

And they remembered me. They had fucked up.

My body ignited a blue glow and my fists were on fire. I felt stronger. With a burning rage within me, I grabbed Vex & Rue by their throats and smashed them together. I lifted my leg to stomp their heads.

"Pare!" Dain yelled, which means, "Stop!"

I looked up and Dain pointed at me as he continued to fight Jr. in the air. Beams of light illuminated their hands, feet and eyes. In a fit of rage, Dain grabbed Jr. and launched him to the ground. "No!" I yelled as Max Jr. fell, landing on top of a sharp piece of metal, and was wedged under it.

"Leve-os para fora!" yelled Jr. to take them out.

I looked and saw Joxel and Zitaya were running toward Taylor. I panicked. I ran toward Taylor. *I feel weaker. I'm slower. They're too far away!* I thought.

The mighty warrior Jaden shot into the air and dashed toward them like a bullet. *Wham! Pow!* Jaden swung and hit Joxel and

Zitaya with his double-sided flaming war hammer. Jaden hit them so hard, he sent them flying a mile away.

Jaden swooped down and grabbed me. We soared through the air to Taylor, who was standing on top of the big dump truck and guarded us. Little Taylor ran into my arms, hugging me tight with teary eyes and looked up at me with a big smile. Kyra flew over to free Tiana.

I felt relieved and ok. I looked around and I realized they had won!

Dain looked right at me with an evil smirk and in that instant, a flash of intense light filled the sky. Dain leapt high into the sky, along with his dark brethren, disappearing into the clouds.

Max Jr. yelled something in an unknown tongue I did not understand.

I looked over at Tiana, distraught and crying, as Camden comforted her. We all flew over to Jr. who lay wounded on the ground. I held Tiana and Taylor. Jr. was carefully freed by his brothers and he stood.

*Woomph!* A powerful gust of wind hit us as Max Jr. displayed his mighty transparent wings. I was again in awe of this mighty Mestre de Batalha, the battle master standing before me, along with all the other angelic warriors. Suddenly my head became clouded and felt dizzy.

Max Jr. then expanded his wings and wrapped them around Tiana, Taylor, and me. We were shrouded in darkness as Max Jr.'s wings engulfed us. My vision blurred and my legs became weak. I looked back up, and to my surprise everything looked normal again. Tiana and Taylor weren't a blur anymore. I looked over at Max Jr., and he too was back to his normal, smaller self. All of them were back to normal.

"Caleb! Are you okay?" Tiana asked.

"Yes. I'm fine. Both my arms hurt. But I'm okay. I'm not

bleeding, am I? Are you and Taylor okay?" I asked. Tiana said
I only had a nosebleed again and they were okay.

I picked up my little girl and she squeezed my neck tight. "It's
okay, honey, everything's okay now, Daddy is here"

"Thank you so much again for saving us. Thank you," Tiana
said to Max Jr.

"How, though?" Tiana asked.

"How what?" I replied.

"How did Max fight so many at once all alone? Max, you're
so fast, the way you fight. I've never seen anything like it. Thank
you again, so much!"

*He fought alone, she said? I fought too. And she did not see his
family there either? What the hell?* I thought.

I looked around and all of Max's family were gone. It was just
the three of us and Max. I looked at Max, baffled, and he gave a
subtle grin.

"You're most welcome Ma'am. It's no problem. I took karate
classes back where I come from. I'm glad you and Taylor are ok,"
said Jr. with an accent.

I pulled Jr. aside and thanked him. I said "When we fought, I
had powers. Like you said. I felt it. But, why did it just go away?
Why could I not fly and do all the other things I saw you and
the others do?"

"This is what I've been trying to tell you. You can do all
those things and more. You're a true bad ass. Now that you have
destroyed what was stopping you, your deceptor, there is nothing
left holding you back. You're almost there. It's time to talk to my
father. You're ready," replied Jr.

Unable to fathom this, I had to find out what was happening to me. I had to know what it all means. I needed to talk to
Maximino Sr. I comforted Tiana, who was still shaken up, telling
her I would explain everything and we headed to Jr.'s.

# 29
## LET'S TALK

WHEN WE GOT to Jr.'s, it was like they knew we were coming, as they greeted us with hugs and warm welcomes. "Rapaz Bonito! He's back everyone," Max Jr. said. I remembered, of course, that means "pretty boy" in Portuguese.

After Maximino Jr. introduced Tiana to everyone he showed us to our room.

"I'll let you guys catch up. My father will be here soon," Jr. said.

I told Tiana I know I'm being shown all of this for a reason. That kid in that dream and the post office lady and now Max and Dain. I opened up and told her everything.

I told her Max said we know each other from another place and that I have powers and he was my new protector and replaced my original one.

"Powers? Protect from who?" Tiana said.

"From Dain."

I told Tiana that Dain was a psychopath killer and the leader of a notorious gang. He's a hit man after me. "Why did he save Taylor and I then? Why did he help you? I don't understand," said Tiana.

"He's a master manipulator from a cult. He's evil, Tiana, and I saw him and his freak family sacrifice a little girl."

Tiana was distraught and said, "Call the damn cops on him already, Caleb! I'm sick of this shit!"

"I'm pretty sure it's going to take more than cops to stop him. Back at the construction site, I saw a lot more. There were others. Max's brothers were there fighting, too. I was also fighting. You didn't see that?"

Tiana replied, "I did see were trying to fight. What do you mean? What else did you see?"

"I was trying to fight? Tiana, listen, I know this sounds crazy. Today, I prayed to God when I almost lost you and Taylor again. When I did, everything and everyone changed! They looked a lot bigger, in angelic-like enchanted armor from another realm. All of them displayed supernatural powers and abilities from out of this world!"

Caleb added, "Max told me I was going to see these things and I did. That's when you and Taylor were saved by Max and his family! He said to unlock my powers I had to remove something called a deceptor and I was going to see even more. You're saying I'm hallucinating? You saw none of this?"

Tiana said, "Caleb, you're scaring me. Why is all of this happening? Why you?"

"It's because I have asked for it. I asked for my purpose."

Tiana hugged me. It was as if she already knew the answer.

"Caleb, I know it's God trying to show you something. Look and listen to what he's telling you, don't fight it, don't think or doubt it anymore."

I smiled and kissed her.

I hugged and kissed little Taylor and Tiana and told them I loved them.

We headed over to the living room with the others.

# 30
## UNMASKED

WE ALL GATHERED around the large living room. I noticed a beautiful white bird in cage. I asked Jr. about the bird. "My father loves that bird," he said.

"It's okay, we will make you happy here," Jr.'s little sister Avary told me.

Jr.'s little brother Brenden said, "I've always believed in you, and I knew you could do it. I'm so happy you're here. My brother." He hugged me and I wept. I could not hold in whatever it was inside another moment.

"Thank you again for everything. Even though all of this is hard to grasp. I now know it means something. Whatever it is, I want to know," I said.

Max Jr. smiled.

"You say your father knows the answer. Is he home now?"

I heard a door open behind me.

"Hello again, Caleb," a calm voice said behind us.

I turned, and to my surprise there was Maximino, Sr., smiling, wearing his signature fedora hat. He walked over and hugged us both. He held out his hand to Taylor, and she held it and smiled. I couldn't explain the instant feeling of comfort Max Sr. gave me, as if I had always known him. From there I didn't hold back.

After telling Max Sr. everything I shook my head and said, "I can't fight it anymore. I know you're a great man of God, and I think it's God himself trying to show me something. Is it my cry to him? Whatever it is, I want to know."

A single tear ran down my cheek from all of the built-up feelings, hurt, and emotions from when I was a child to now, as Tiana hugged and comforted me.

Max Sr. smiled, placed his hand on my shoulder, and said, "Caleb, I have heard your heart, and have felt your faith without a single word." He looked at Max Jr. and said, "Son, show him."

We walked to their large backyard full of broken-down vehicles and equipment with an oil rig in the middle. Max Jr. pointed high up to the oil rig and said, "Well, Rapaz Bonito, this is it. The answer to what you're looking for is up there. Climb to the top."

I looked and replied, "Up there? You've got to be joking."

I could tell he wasn't kidding. "Shit! I guess it's a bad time to mention I hate heights, huh?"

I looked at Tiana, who gave me a nod of encouragement. I began climbing to the top.

I reached the top, and it was an awesome sight. I could see for miles. "Babe, are you okay?" Tiana yelled.

I looked down and my heart sank when I realized how high I was. I must have been a hundred feet high or more.

"Don't look here, look there!" said Jr. and pointed to the sky. "Don't look down! Look up!" Max Jr. yelled. My heart started beating fast, and my breathing intensified. It was like I wanted to jump out of my skin, as a warm feeling hit me. Instantly, I had no worry, no doubt or any care whatsoever, as I simply shut it all out. It was as if I'd put my single finger to my lips and shushed everything. I had stopped the entire world that surrounded me, and looked up to the clouds and sky.

"Close your eyes!" Max Jr. yelled. And so I did. When I did, however, it was like a slow blink as a gentle breeze hit my face. I felt a peace like I'd never felt, and I began to cry.

I opened my eyes again and I was dumbfounded. I looked around and I could see everything, the entire city was so close to me, as if it all was in 3D! Not just this city, either—I could see many cities, for miles and miles around me, and all the people in them!

I saw everything happening from all around as the people went about their everyday lives. Some people were walking and others were driving cars. There were some people riding bikes and others on buses and trains. I could even see the people's faces in the windows of planes above, as well as the ones inside the buildings and houses below. There were so many people, and all of them I could see in great detail, as if I were standing right next to them!

"Yeah! Wahoo! Go! Go!"

*What's that?* I thought, startled, hearing people so close. I turned, and it was the celebration from a football game going on in a stadium a few cities away.

*How, though? I heard the cheering right next to me*, I thought, confused. Over there were more cheers, from a concert. To my left was more loud applause at a fashion show, and behind me the jeers of a bodybuilding championship. I could see a video game tournament happening in Los Angeles and other loud celebrations at a huge church building in front of me.

I could see it all, from Las Vegas to Chicago to the ring of the bell at the stock exchange in New York. *Woomph!* I dashed high up into the sky and found myself levitating in midair among the clouds. Louder and louder, the cheers intensified, from all of the events.

*Wait!* I realized I could see the entire world! From a political rally in Beijing, China, to an amusement park in Belgium, Germany, I could see and hear it all happening at once, as if I were standing right next to everything!

*How can this be?* I thought.

That's when I noticed something else. Everyone was completely immersed in their cellphones and electronics as they walked, drove, and flew. All of them were affixed to their devices, as if on autopilot. Somehow, the mere sight of this was disturbing. *Why am I being shown this? What does it all mean?* I wondered. I was quickly reminded again, asking myself, *Is this what life's all about? Is this really all we're living for? There has got to be more to living, just to die.*

I blinked a second time and when I looked again I was baffled, as everything changed even more. Everything is now a greyish color, just as in my dreams, with that young boy.

*What's this?* I wondered. Now I could see other large, dark figures in black, transparent robes. They were all over, along with those other larger ones in white garments, amongst the people, just as in my dreams. The ones in dark appear to be seeking out all the people.

I looked closer and noticed some of the dark seekers were walking along the sides of some people, having conversations with them, as if they knew them. There were other seekers standing next to some of the people, while other seekers randomly dashed toward others, as if stalking them. It was as if all the people were being pursued by these mysterious figures.

That was when I noticed something else. Those figures in white were also pursuing the people to help them. The ones in white were trying to prevent the dark figures from engaging the people.

*What are the white and dark figures doing?* I wondered. There were many of these seekers outnumbering the ones in white, at least ten to one. I saw dark figures hanging onto the sides of buildings, and others were on rooftops and on houses, peeking in the windows as if looking for something. Other dark figures were on the tops of moving cars, buses, and trains, while many others were hanging on the outside of planes in the sky. I could see all of this happening all over the world.

*Wait! The people! They don't even realize or see all the dark and white figures all around them. It's like they're invisible.* Everyone was oblivious to these figures, or anything that happened around them, yet I could see them all. "What are they doing to them?" I cringed to see some of the dark figures were latched onto some of the people. They were actually clinging to the backs and fronts of the them!

*Oh my God!* I thought in shock, realizing the top halves of these dark figures were literally sticking out of some of the people. They were half-infused inside of them with only their arms and heads sticking out. They were like leeches, conversing and pointing directions with the people, guiding them as they went about their lives. *What are these among the people, angels?* I wondered. I became distraught, to see the impact these dark figures had. The seekers lurked and preyed over the people, hovering over their heads as they roamed aimlessly.

*Some people can see them?* I wondered. *Yes! I can see some of the them are able to see some of the figures. These dark robed fuckers are guiding and controlling the people! Turning them into self-gratifying, animalistic devourers of life.* I saw some dark seekers talking to political and military leaders, influencing them to make war for their own twisted agendas.

Other dark seekers were convincing and guiding corrupt church leaders and high politicians to mislead the people. I saw other dark seekers persuading corporations, stealing money and creating bogus schemes. Other seekers made deals with business executives, convincing them to defraud innocent people and manipulate the make-believe stock market. They robbed them all for their own financial gain. Everyone from the White House, to the people in their homes, to all the people around the world, are plagued by these evil figures in black.

They stalked the clueless, roaming people, giving each person their own personal downfall, targeting their weaknesses. The seekers were doing everything from lighting others' cigarettes with addicted smokers, to giving drugs to addicts of all ages. Other seekers were toasting alcohol with alcoholics, and pushing food onto the gluttonous and obese, while other seekers took food away from the disordered and the poor. Clothes, jewelry, and material things of all kinds were pushed and made a focus to all, only to have the people want more.

These seekers promised power, fame, fortune, and magical wonders to the people. I could hear the dark seekers negotiating masterfully, convincing the people. I could hear it as if I were standing right next to them. It was like I could see the sad and sickening end result to everyone. All of it was designed to deceive and feed an unquenchable thirst for greed, power, and a lust for life—a life that would end in destruction. A feeling of disgust and rage consumed me. I felt my fists got hot. I have to do something!

Out of the masses I focused on a young girl walking on top of a bridge. She walked over to the edge and looked over. I noticed a seeker next to her, who leaned over and whispered something in her ear.

"No!" I screamed in horror as the young girl jumped to her death. In that apartment over there was a young boy who injected a drug into his arm. He was handed another dose from a dark one as the boy gladly accepted. For the last time, the boy shot up, overdosed, and died.

Everyone was listening to these fucks! They were all doing exactly as they said, while they gave whispers of death with a smile.

All of these dark seekers were tormenting the people while

causing belief arguments, fighting, stealing, and killing of all forms. They stirred up an unrelenting rage throughout the world, turning all of humanity against itself, fueling the wrath of political leaders, biker gangs, drug cartels, and gangs of all kinds. The seekers forced the hands of governments and presidents to war with other countries, while stirring hatred among the people, causing riots and race wars.

All this while the seekers participate in music videos, movie screenings, and world events, celebrating in a mocking fashion, right in front of the blind people as if distracting them. Everyone was being used like puppets, as they cheered, laughed, and praised the carnage they created throughout the world. "Oh, yes! Help them, dammit!" I yelled in frustration to the figures in white, who were trying to stop the dark seekers. The ones in dark were even morphing into the forms of people with great deception, while possessing others.

I saw these dark figures took the forms of young children and the elderly, and the drunken homeless who lay on the side of the road. I even saw a tiny baby suddenly walk around a corner, and morph into a demonic figure. The ones in white were desperately trying to stop and protect the people. Even though the light figures were greatly outnumbered, they still fought vigorously to guard and protect the people from the ones in dark. The ones in white were only helping some of the people, though, not all of them, for some reason.

*They can't win. They're losing!* I thought.

The dark watchers of the people preyed on them mercilessly. They caused all forms of horrendous evilness, pitting the people against each other. *They are killing all of humanity!* I thought. Enraged, I lunged to grab one of the dark seekers as they flew by, and went right through them. My heart sank, and I was filled with sadness, realizing I was helpless in the face of the chaos around me.

I blinked a third time and felt my heart stop. I was blinded by a piercing flash and began to fall to the ground below.

"Ah!" I kicked and swung my hands wildly as I fell, and screamed in horror. *Woomph!* I shot right back up, hovering once again in midair as my sight returned. When I looked again, I gasped. I was now looking at another realm entirely. Everyone and everything was illuminated with such intense, majestic radiance, it took my breath away. I looked to the ground below Maximino Jr., who was back in his mighty epic form, in battle stance. His epic, transparent wings were widespread with beams of intense light projecting from his eyes.

All of the dark and light figures were now transformed into mighty, enchanted warriors. All the light guardians and dark seekers were viciously fighting each other in the air, on the ground, and in the sea. The light guardians fought riding on the backs of majestic horses with eyes of blue fire. The dark seekers fought, riding on sinister and demonic horses, bears, and wolves with beaming eyes. Every animal was nothing I had ever seen before. Almost humanoid, all of the animals were fighting vigorously.

With brute force, all of them bucked, kicked, and swung their hooves, claws, and tails, with electric surges as they hit. There were others who fought in the sea, as the dark seekers rode on enchanted, battle-hardened, demonic sharks and fierce stingrays with red eyes and fire about them. The guardians rode on enchanted, battle-hardened seahorses and dolphins, who launched powerful ripple surges of water with swings of their tails.

I even saw others fighting in the sky, as they rode inside the clouds. They rode clouds as chariots with bolts of fire surging throughout the cloud.

Suddenly, total darkness covered the land. I looked down, and noticed an enormous shadow. I looked up and saw a massive cloud overhead, and stumbled back.

I realized the cloud was alive! It was a giant electric cloud warrior.

There were enormous cloud warriors, with blue bolts of fire surging through them, as the others had black bolts of fire, clashing overhead. "Oh my God," I uttered in fear. Below were all the people, the roamers, who were in blurred forms, as Tiana and Taylor were back at the construction site. All I could see were the people's faces in a blurred bubble as the mighty warriors battled all around them.

The ferocious battle was unfathomable to witness as intense beams of light and fire flew back and forth, covering the sky. Every living thing on the planet, in the air, on the land, and in the sea, was now in a mighty majestic form, battling relentlessly. It was an all-out war!

The trees, were mighty, majestic warriors that fired enchanted leaves that were alive themselves. The trees' leaves were live mini-drones, vigorously seeking out their targets. The birds launched fiery talons, as the tiniest of ants shot electric beams from their antennae. The fireflies were now fierce and mighty, projecting laser-like beams from their eyes.

Every small, timid creature and animal we knew of was now an enchanted, battle-hardened warrior. The fish launched blue bolts of fire from their fins, while the eels, jellyfish, and plants projected intense laser-like rays into the sea. Everything from the smallest insect to the largest animal transformed into an epic battle form, fighting alongside the mighty angelic warriors to the death.

"Help them! Why aren't you helping them all? We're losing!" I yelled at Maximino Jr., who remained still. The sounds of grunts and clashes intensified around me as the devastating carnage con-tinued. Unable to take it, I closed my eyes. "Caleb!" a voice yelled from below me. I looked down, and it was Tiana!

I found myself standing back on top of the oil rig. Everything was back to normal. "Are you okay? Caleb, come down!" Tiana yelled again. I sighed in relief.

I was in great shock and frightened by all I had just witnessed, and began sweating profusely. I hurried down the rig's ladder, and rushed over to Tiana, hugging her tightly. I was unable to hold back all of the emotions as tears streamed down my cheeks. We all headed back inside, where I shared my experience on top of the oil rig. Upon hearing it all, Tiana began to cry.

"You really are angels, aren't you?" Max Jr. looked back at me, and to my surprise he said without his thick accent, "Caleb, we have no time to waste. Now that you've been enlightened to this revelation, Dain will quickly find out. And the second he learns of this; he will come after you with everything he's got."

I felt my heart skip a beat, hearing this. Max Jr. said "Only together will we be able to beat him. Before we can defeat Dain, however, there is one last thing we must overcome."

"One last thing? How much more of this can one take? Who, or what are you guys?"

For some reason Jr. Looked down at my feet.

# 31

# A WALK ABOVE

DEEP BUZZ echoed the room, and my feet became as cold as icicles. I looked down at my feet and noticed the carpet. *What's this? The carpet is suddenly another color, and it's moving? It's dirt!* I thought, frightened. "What the hell is going on here?" I said.

I looked up and found myself outside somewhere. All around me was a vast, gray wasteland.

*How can this be?* I wondered. *Tiana and Taylor! Where are they? Is it that dream again? I'm not sleeping, though!*

Unable to comprehend what was happening, I looked around. The screeching of the wind pierced my ears. I looked to my left, then to my right. Nothing for miles. I look behind me to only see more dirt, sticks, and rocks. Tumbleweeds roll here and there, and I see hills and bushes for miles. My feet started to hurt.

I was barefoot. *What the hell am I wearing?* Some sort of a gray, raggedy, sleeveless covering. I heard howls from animals in the distance, as dust clouds surrounded me. I felt my stomach sink as I realized I was utterly alone.

I walked around, to explore this strange land, and I noticed something moving in the other direction. I felt as if I'm being watched. *Is it a person over there, next to that hill?* Cautiously, I headed over for a closer look.

A person was standing there. *A kid?* To my surprise, it was a young, dark-skinned boy, sitting alone next to a cliff. *What's a kid doing in the middle of nowhere? He must be lost and scared. And why is he sitting so close to that cliff?* I walked over to him. He was staring down at something. "Hey there, little buddy," I said in a soft, calm voice.

The boy jumped up, frightened, and looked back at me. "Oh, hi," he said with a stare. The young boy turned back around, and again looked downward.

Just like that, the boy sat back down, as If I wasn't even there. I mean, this kid was so close to that cliff edge it made me uncomfortable. "Hey there, it's going to be all right. Why are you so close to that edge there? Are you okay? You should scoot back some." The little boy continued to look down, with no response.

*Something is not right. There's no telling what he may do.* I kept my distance. "What's your name?" I asked.

"I'm Rel," the boy replied, not looking back.

"Hey, I'm Caleb. Nice to meet you."

Rel continued looking down the cliff as I asked, "Where are your parents? And what is this place?"

Rel replied, "They're around."

*What does that mean?* I look around and see there's nothing close by for miles.

I heard something in the distance. It sounded like faint laughter and cheering, just over that hill. Curious, I walked over and stepped up on a boulder, to see what it was. While I was standing on the big rock, I heard louder, distant cheers and chatter.

I heard a crash behind me. I looked back and saw, through all the dull greyness, a big, bright, and colorful city in the far distance. The massive city was glowing, and stood out in this dark and gloomy land that surrounded it.

I marveled at the city's vibrant colors, and I saw a wide pathway leading toward it. And on this single path, heading to the city, were many, many people coming from one direction.

I noticed, in the opposite direction, a small, dark city, with no path leading to it. This smaller place blended in with the gray surroundings and was hard to see. Like the other city, there were also people heading toward it. However, there were only a few people going there. And they were coming from many directions, all around it.

I looked back at Rel, and I could see he was still sitting there, looking downward. I walked back over to him, determined to know what all this meant. "Those two cities over there, what are those places?" I asked Rel.

Again, he gave no response. He was even closer to the edge than before. *Is this kid really thinking jumping off it?* I wondered.

"Rel, please. Move back from there, you don't have to do this. Give me your hand," I said, with my hand outstretched. Rel looked back at me with a blank stare, no emotion, and turned back once again.

*What the hell is this kid doing? What does he keep staring at?* I walked over next to him and leaned over for a look.

I leaned over a little more, and, "Oh shit! Shit!" I screamed in horror. I jumped back, to see there was nothing but clouds and sky. *We're floating in midair! How can this be?* I fell to my hands and knees. Clearly, we had to be high on some overhanging mountain. I carefully leaned over once more, all the way, for a closer look.

"Oh my God! Oh God!" I yelled, jumping back.

We were on some sort of floating island. I got on my hands and knees, trying to regain control of myself, and make sense of this. Rel looked at me with concern, and I asked, "Are we really floating?"

Rel replied, "Don't worry. You're going to be okay. We're going back."

I hate heights. I leaned over for another look and saw nothing but a lot of clouds, and a few birds. Nothing but sky. Puzzled, I asked Rel, "Where are we going back to? And what do you keep looking at? There's nothing. Am I missing something?"

Rel looked at me, then looked back down as he pointed downward. I looked again, even closer. And there, through the thick clouds and flying birds, I could see what appeared to be ants. Like an ant colony.

It was like a million of little ants, crawling all around. I asked, "Are those ants you keep looking at?" Without a word, Rel pointed downward again. Once again, I looked, and as I did, I could not believe my eyes. Suddenly it all became crystal clear. It was as if I looked through binoculars that zoomed in on everything. Those little ants weren't ants at all, they're people! Below us was some sort of place with what seemed like millions and millions of people.

*How can this be? I can see each person in detail as before on the oil rig.* I grabbed a nearby shrub root to hold onto as I leaned down for a closer look.

"Who are those people down there?" I asked Rel.

"They're Roamers," Rel replied.

"Roamers?"

When I looked again, it was all familiar. *I've seen this before!* They weren't all the same. Some of the figures were larger than others.

I noticed the larger ones were darker and the smaller ones were lighter. The darker ones seemed to be following the lighter ones. Then I noticed something else, as a lot of the lighter ones that were followed by the bigger suddenly disappeared—as if they were grabbed by the dark ones and made to vanish. I saw them being chased and, just like that, they were gone.

Yes! Those darker figures are taking those other ones. The dark ones are literally grabbing the ones in white and dragging them away I thought. "What's going on here Rel? What am I looking at?" I asked sternly. Rel looks at me and replies "The ones you no longer see have been taken to their chosen place in time."

*A place in time?* I thought.

I asked Rel, "Who are those larger, darker figures? And who are those other lighter ones in white robes among those roamers?"

Rel responded, "The ones in dark are Trydentiums. The ones in light are Lytenials."

I didn't know what that meant. All I knew was, it sounded like some deep, serious shit.


"What is that place down there?" I asked Rel, who turned around and said something I didn't understand. "I'm sorry, say that again?" I replied. All I heard was screeching wind gusts which echoed in my ear. I looked at the strange land of emptiness around me.

# 32

# COME ON IN

I WAS IN the midst of nowhere. I looked again in the distance, at that small, dark, desolate city. And in the opposite direction was that big, colorful, glowing city.

*What are these places?* I wondered again.

The bright, colorful city continued to draw me to it. I couldn't resist it any longer. I started to walk toward it.

Out of a nowhere, I heard, "Don't do it, mister. It's rough there. It's bad…"

I looked behind me, and it was that young kid, Rel.

"What do you mean? What's over there that's so bad?"

Rel didn't respond.

Despite Rel telling me not to go, I wanted to find out and know what was over there. I couldn't resist the allure of the bright and colorful city that was so inviting another moment as I continued towards it. "I think I'll take my chances, little buddy. I'll be all right. You really should get home. I'm sure your parents are worried about now," I said while walking away.

"No. you won't be all right," Rel responded.

I looked back at Rel and asked, "I won't be?"

I walked toward the large city, and noticed Rel shaking his head as he looked at the ground. It was as if he was bothered or pondering something. To my surprise, Rel started to follow me, as I continued ahead anyway. I started to think this kid was maybe not all there, and knew I had to be on guard.

A little way down the rocky dirt road, I looked back and noticed Rel suddenly stopped and turned around back in the direction we came from.

He just stood there for a moment, staring down the hilly road. I looked a little farther down the hill and saw three figures wearing black. They walked up the hill towards us slowly. Rel stood there in the middle of the road as they walked up and stopped a few feet away. Concerned, I started to head over to the kid, who stood there motionless. Suddenly Rel started to backpedal away from the three who were coming in my direction. I knew this couldn't be good. Rel looked at me for a second and turned back to the mysterious figures.

In the blink of an eye, Rel expanded epic blue transparent wings, trimmed of white fire. *He's an angel?* I wondered. He leapt into a spinning spear punch, hitting one of them in the face, knocking them to the ground. The other two charged at Rel, who dodged so fast I couldn't believe my eyes.

That little boy launched a barrage of lightning-fast kicks and punches like I'd never seen. Rel grabbed a rock and threw it at the face of one of them as blood splattered, knocking them to the ground. Rel leapt into a spinning roundhouse, kicking the other one, knocking them to the ground. Rel jumped high over the head of the downed figure, stomping on his face, killing him.

"Oh, no! No!" I yelled as one of the dark figures pulled out what looked like a glowing slingshot and fired it. I heard the whiff of it being fired, hitting Rel in the head, knocking him back to the ground. The other dark figure teleported over, grabbed Rel, and swung him like a rag doll, smashing him to the ground repeatedly. He threw him against a boulder. "Stop! Please!" I cried out. Rel was covered in blood as he struggled to get up. He sat up and coughed blood.

I ran as fast as I could to Rel's aid.

I could see the two dark figures standing over the motionless Rel. "Hey! What the fuck are you doing?" The two dark figures looked at me for a few seconds. I ran faster. "He's just a kid! Leave him alone! You're going to kill him!"

The two dark figures turned to each other, and just like that they walked away in a cloud of mist. I rushed over to Rel, who was lying in a pool of blood. I grabbed him in my arms "Rel! Are you okay?" He didn't respond.

I held Rel's limp body. *He's not breathing!* I began to tear up. Blood poured from his mouth and nose. I tried to revive him, but it was hopeless. There was no mistaking it; Rel was dead.

*This poor little kid, how can this be? What the hell just happened here?* I wiped my tears away.

I heard a crash. I turned around and saw someone in a grey robe walking over. I stood and the figure said, "No, it's okay. I mean you no harm. He was my friend." The man walked over.

The peculiar man leaned over Rel's lifeless body and knelt down with one knee with his head bowed. I could see the man was very saddened as he deeply grieved for Rel. "I'm Nehriol, a good friend of Rel's. I'm sorry you had to see this" the man said and stood up. "I'm Caleb, nice to meet you. Why did they kill him? He's just a little boy."

Nehriol replied, "I know. It's a tragedy and never should have happened."

"Who were those people?" I asked.

"They will pay for this. We will avenge Rel. We will need help, as there are many of them."

"Many? Where are they? In fact, I beg you, where the hell am I? What's happening here?"

"Come. I'll show you. We need to go for help," Nehriol replied as he headed toward the colorful city. I followed.

"We're just going to leave him here? We can't just leave him," I said.

Nehriol replied, "Yes. We will come back. The city—it's safe there. They will help us."

As we got closer, I noticed parts of the ground had large and small holes or openings revealing the sky below. I was again reminded that we were floating in midair. I looked up to see in the distance three dark, glowing figures heading to the big city.

*Are they hovering?* I wondered. They were. They were all gliding fast across the desolate wasteland.

I turned and noticed three other dark figures leaving the big city from another direction. I looked to the small, grey city in the opposite direction and saw three more strange figures leaving it. *Where are they all going?* I wondered. When I looked down again, through one of the large openings, I couldn't believe what I saw. There were others ascending from that other city Rel was looking at, far below.

"Oh shit!" I said, seeing some of the dark figures jumping through the openings, flying toward the city below. We got closer to the vibrant city ahead, and I saw more of the mysterious figures in black robes. They were roaming in groups of three, to and from the three different places: the big, bright city ahead, the small grey city behind us, and the city far below us.

"And what is this place?" He didn't respond. "I'm dead, aren't I?"

Nehriol responded, "You are not."

Looking around this vast, grey wasteland, I noticed a few scattered figures that were all alone. Just like the others, they were gliding across the land, traveling to and from all three cities. These, however, wore all white garments and moved more slowly.

"Don't worry. We will get the help we need there," Nehriol said, pointing to the bright city ahead. "Everything will make sense and be okay once we're there."

# 33
## NOT TODAY

"THIS WAY. WE'RE almost there..." Nehriol said.

I could see the city ahead and was much larger than I'd thought it was. I heard laughter and cheers getting louder. I was awestruck by the sheer structure and beauty that surrounded me. The grand designs and markings of the tapestries that hung over the walls were glowing. Everything from the statues, decorations to the mighty guards, had a glow of enchantment around them.

The size of this place and its vibrancy were breathtaking. The guards were huge and intimidating to look upon. They wore enchanted white battle-hardened armor with glowing blue gleaming underlining, and blue beaming eyes. The guards watched our every step as we passed them.

"What is this place?" I asked.

Nehriol replied, "The city of Anulace. We will be safe here. Help is inside."

I was anxious and excited. I was greeted with nods and smiles from the people who welcomed me in. They were celebrating and cheering my arrival. It was as if they expected me.

As we walked through the courtyard, I was awestruck. The streets were made of gold, the plants gave off a glow as they moved, and the fountains streamed water that glistened in the daylight. The statues and tapestries were of emerald and sapphire that gleamed brightly, illuminating the city.

I saw even more people heading into the great city, smiling and laughing as they went inside. I suddenly felt safe and assured here at this grand city.

A group of others rushed over to Nehriol, and communicated in some other strange tongue, and they headed inside. Nehriol turned back to me with a smile and said, "Welcome, Caleb, to Anulace"

All I could think about was that young boy, Rel.

"We can't just leave him there; we have to go back and get him!" I said to Nehriol in frustration.

Nehriol replied, "No. We can't go back, there will be more. We need help."

*There will be more? More of the ones that killed him?* I thought.

As we walked up to the front gates, I looked behind me, down the hill, where Rel was lying, and noticed another figure in white garments standing next to him.

My view was blocked by two other figures in white, who greeted Nehriol. "Did you see any more of them? How many?" Nehriol asked the two figures.

"Yes, there are many over the hill, heading this way," one of the figures replied.

I looked back at Rel, and the other figure next to him, and to my surprise the figure was gone. They had taken Rel!

"Quick! We must hurry into the city for help, we don't have much time! Hurry, Caleb, now," Nehriol insisted.

I felt uneasy. When I looked back again, however, the two

figures in white prevented me, rushing us to the city's main gates just ahead. *Whack!* I felt something hit my foot. I looked down to see a faintly glowing rock roll by.

The others ahead didn't notice the rock as it rolled off to the right into a bush. The bush was now glowing, drawing me to it. I walked over to the bush and moved the branches, looking for the rock inside.

When I looked into the bush, I was in disbelief. It was as if I were looking through a window to another place. There, inside the bush, I saw a person in white garments, getting the shit kicked out of them. The person in white was getting jumped by a group of others in all black robes.

This person was not even trying to defend them self. They were just lying there, as the other ones in black savagely kicked and hit them. *Why does all of this look so familiar? I've seen all this before. Why aren't they fighting back?* I thought.

"Hey! They're going to kill another one! They're going to kill him!" I yelled.

Nehriol replied, "We can't help. There are too many. Hurry inside, Caleb! We must go through the gates!"

*Something is off.* A bright light flashed from the bush and I looked inside again. This time, the bloodied and battered person in white turned and looked right at me.

It was Maximino Jr.! The hair stood on my neck. At this moment I recalled Rel, who told me the ones in dark, the watchers, would pressure, force, and take. The ones in white would not, as they would help only when welcomed or when asked. I turned back to Nehriol and the others, who were heading toward me. The ones in white before me were not what they seemed.

It was only now, I confirmed Jr.'s words, that I watched Rel, my own guardian angel, die before my eyes. Now Maximino Jr. had to replace him. I could have prevented it. I know I could have fought and saved Rel. He died for my lack of belief!

My breathing intensified. I felt a burning rage stir within.

*Both of them were with me the whole time, trying to tell me all of this. And now Rel died because of me!*

*I know where my belief lies. Jr. was right, I do know who I am. And, I know where I am. I'm home.*

My fists went hot and ignited into blue flames.

I looked back into the bush, at the broken and battered Max Jr., who was already looking up at me. It was as if he were waiting for me and my direction. All of sudden, I felt the most intense channeling of my entire being connected with him, as I gave a nod of assurance of faith.

This change, this affirmation within my spirit, fueled Maximino Jr., giving him strength, instantly turning us both into merciless destroyers.

Inside the bush, Max Jr. struck back viciously, catching the group of demons off-guard, killing them. I looked behind and stumbled back to see Nehriol and the other two figures in white running at me, now only a few feet away. Immediately, an intense ray of light illuminated from the big bush, stunning Nehriol and the other two. A bolt of light from the bush shot out, hitting me, knocking me to the ground.

Dazed, I hurried back to my feet and couldn't believe my eyes. Nehriol and the other two figures changed! They were all now in black robes with demonic grins. The entire city of Anulace transformed into a dark, wicked place of despair. Shrieks and cries of torment and suffering were all around. The stench of death and decay was overwhelming. "Mestre de Batalha!" I heard one of the dark demons yell and hissed, while pointing behind me.

"Kill him!" Nehriol yelled.

*Pow!* Out of nowhere, Maximino Jr. spearheaded right into the two demons, knocking them to the ground, engaging them in fierce battle. Max Jr. swiftly killed the two devil angelics, and struggled with the mighty Nehriol.

"Caleb! He's a Ceifador! A soul reaper, war god…he will kill me!"

I shot in the air and pummeled Nehriol, pounding him with fists of fire. Each of my blows ignited like bombs. Nehriol knocked us back with a burst of energy. A deafening screech pierced our ears behind us. I looked and saw it was a demonic woman appear from a black mist.

"Ceifeira! She's a reaper witch! Don't be afraid of her Caleb, she feeds of fear and will enter you," yelled Jr.

Nehriol began channeling a red energy force around him and conjured minions from the ground made of dirt. He grasped a whip of black fire and swung, wrapping it around us, and slammed us to the ground. The Ceifador's power was too great.

Nehriol's eyes turned black. "No!" yelled Jr.

I felt weak and could not move suddenly. A black beam of energy shot into our mouths. He began to drain our souls.

Out of nowhere, another light guardian intervened, aiding us. And I knew who this other guardian was. It wasn't Max's brother, but the fierce and mighty archangelic, Michael! He threw his mighty sword of light, and knocked Nehriol to the ground. All three of us viciously beat down the war god Nehriol, who managed to escape into a black cloud of mist.

I looked up at the bloodied Maximino Jr., and Michael and gave my nod of approval. I turned around, away from the darkness of Anulace, and headed down the path toward the smaller, grey city and noticed a familiar large tree in the center. Jr. and Michael followed.

Before my very eyes, the small grey and desolate city changed into a mighty city of wonder. It gleamed with great, majestic splendor, even more than the false city of Anulace of old. I headed down the new path toward the mighty city.

I turned back to Jr. and Michael and they were gone. I faced the new, bright city ahead. "Caleb! Caleb!" a voice yelled.

"Huh?" I said, when I heard the familiar voice. *The voice came from the ground?*

I looked to the ground and noticed it had opened. I knelt down and carefully looked through the hole. It was Tiana! And, there was Taylor! Someone one was dragging them away by their arms. *What the hell?* I thought. Both Tiana and Taylor were trying to get away, crying and kicking while reaching up toward me. "No! Stop!" I yelled.

The person dragging them slowly turned around. Glaring back at me with a wicked smirk was Dain! "Oh my God! No! Stop!" I screamed, and reached for them.

Suddenly, the entire ground underneath me opened and I fell into the sky. Unable to look, I kicked and screamed in horror, free-falling to the unknown below.

I opened my eyes and found myself back on the couch at the Montez's house. "Caleb, you're fine, you're okay. You zoned out a few minutes. Jr's talking to you and you weren't responding," Tiana said. I felt my heart race and hugged Tiana and Taylor, relieved they were okay.

Still shaken, I looked at Sr. and Jr. And said, "What did I just see? Who are you?

With a nod, Max Jr. said, "We are Lytenials, from the Lytenial tree-line. We're Guardiaos in this world, guardians here for our brethren. I am a high archangelic known as Mestre de Batalha, an elite battle-master. As mentioned, prior, I have been assigned to you, in place of our brother, Rel, who was on trial to become a Mestre de Batalha. Was this now revealed to you? What did you see?"

"Yes, Rel! I was back in that grey wasteland again. Now I know it was no dream. Those fuckers killed him in cold blood! I saw it with my own eyes. Rel is the one who told me about the Lytenials. You are the ones Rel spoke of when I was on the floating city. And you're the one I thought I saw when I looked back again, who was kneeling next to Rel, weren't you?"

Max Jr. held his head low and said, "It was Nehriol who killed him."

I pounded my fists in anger.

Max Jr. said, "Our enemy are the Trydentiums, from the Trydentium tree-line. They're watchers here on this earth, dark seekers called Buscadors."

I replied, "You truly are angels. And that's who Dain and his family are, they're all Trydentiums! I knew that Mirtaza gang story was pure bullshit! I also noticed differently colored wings on the angelics. Why?".

"Yes. All angelics reflect their hierarchy through wing color: grey are the unchosen ones, lost in the void of time. White is a recruit. Blue is a battle-hardened veteran, with red trim or white being the elder. Red is a battle master, with white trim or black being the elder. Black is an Arco de Batalha, high arch-angelic of hosts. When enraged, all angelics will reflect their wing trim ablaze. The fallen, Trydentiums, have the same mirrored abilities and powers to us, their counterparts."

It was what Max. Jr. said next that shook me to the core. "Dain is also a high archangelic. He's one of the high elders. Dain had become one of the most powerful Mestre de Batalhas there ever were, but he defected. He was my mentor and my older brother."

Jr. added, "He has since become the highest dark angelics to ever exist. During the sacred trials of hosts, we battled in front of all angelics from both sides. I was the only one called and chosen to challenge him. As you know, I lost. Total devastation was all I felt. I'm still in shock."

Maximino Jr. continued and said, "I failed everyone, and let my father down. Mocked by all Trydentiums and disgraced. Dain is my bitter enemy, and the only one I've been unable to defeat."

"Why me?"

Max Sr. replied, "Because, prior to here, you have chosen your place in time. You're of our bloodline, Caleb. You're one of us."

"Now it's Dain who's also assigned to you. And, he will not stop until your destroyed."

I looked into Jr's eyes. I said, "Destroy me? Nah. Not today."

I held Taylor and Tiana. "God is truly with us, Tiana. Tomorrow, we're going to finish this."

# 34

# ON A CLOUD

IT WAS THE next morning and we wasted no time. We all knew I was ready to face Dain. This time I would not be alone. We devised a plan to go back to Dain, under the premise of surrendering to his god. Before Dain, I would give myself to Lucio, in order to keep my family from harm.

With our plan set, I drove down the familiar deserted road to Dain's house. "Shit! I don't have time for this!" I yelled. I saw flashes behind me and pulled over. Through the review mirror I saw a male and female police officer, wearing shades, walking up to each side of my car. "Is there a problem, officer?" I asked.

"Yes, there is. A big one…" the male officer replied in a familiar voice.

*What the shit?* I thought, while I looked to the officer standing on my left. The officer slowly leaned down, into my driver-side window, and removed his sunglasses

It was Joxel! I looked to the other side—it was Zitaya! I knew I had to keep cool, and stick to the plan. "You guys get a part-time job or something? Believe it or not, I was just on my way to your house. Where's Dain? I want to talk to him," I said.

"Yes, first day. Now cut the bullshit. You would have just ran again otherwise. Where's your friend, Jr.?" Joxel asked.

I said, "Your brother was right. Maximino is a traitor. I found out a lot of things about him, and Dain has to know now."

They grinned. Zitaya walked over to my door with Joxel.

Joxel chuckled. He said, "C'mon now. You really don't think we believe that, do you?"

I got out of the car and casually placed my arms around both. I smiled. I looked into their blank stares and smashed their heads together. They dropped.

"Nope," I replied.

*Not a thought. I had done that.*

*So much for playing it cool.*

As I pulled into the driveway, Dain and the rest of his family were already outside, waiting. The sky was clear, and on this day I knew the light shined on me. I got out of the car, and walked over to Dain, instantly feeling a dark presence.

"Well, look who it is. We have a visitor, my family," Dain said. He exhaled a puff of smoke from his joint, adding, "Change your mind? Caleb… C'mon. You know me better than that. I know why you're here. And we're ready."

"Sorry, boy, you already lost. You fell for their lies, just like I once did. Only for you, it's too late. I can sense the fear and confusion all over you. Now, you're going to pay with your soul as you stand there, alone," Dain said with a wicked smirk.

I scowled and felt my fists burn. I looked into his eyes, I thought, *Yeah Dain, there you go. I know you see it now. My fury.*

"Who said I was alone?" I replied.

Dain's eyes grew large, and his face turned pale white. Dain went ballistic, swearing in an unknown language, as his dark brethren stood next to him, perplexed.

A black mist appeared behind Dain. "Now you will witness the power of the one and only true god. Behold, the power of my god!" Dain yelled. A familiar breeze hit my face, and I felt a hand touch my right shoulder. I looked, and it was Max Jr., who stood by my side. He was looking up to the sky. I looked up and saw a cloud, with two fierce-looking light angelics, heading right for me. The two striking angelics illuminated in majestic white armor and transparent red wings trimmed with white fire and beaming white eyes.

"Arqueiros, elite arch host angelics," said Jr.

I couldn't believe my eyes as the cloud engulfed me, lifting me into the air. Higher and higher I went, escorted by Max Jr. and the other two angelics on each side.

High above, past the clouds, appeared an entirely different place. It was as if we went through a portal, into a vast land from another realm. The cloud I was riding on descended to the land below, and rested me on a pinnacle as the cloud vanished. There I was, standing with Max Jr. and the two other elite angelics, overlooking a landscape.

I looked over at Maximino Jr., who now appeared in his epic, radiant angelic battle form. I began breathing heavily. Max Jr. looked at me and nodded, and suddenly he and the other two angelics flew to the ground below. I looked to the other side, across from Max Jr. and the two angelics, and saw a black mist appear.

Out of the black mist ascended the Trydentiums in their epic dark angelic forms, followed by Dain Stone. They all stood directly across from Max Jr. and the two elite Arqueiros. *What is happening here? Is this another one of those battle of host trials Max Jr. spoke of? It's fifteen vs. three?* I looked all around, only to realize there were no other Lytenials.

*Max is going to be slaughtered!*

Without hesitation, Max Jr. bolted right at Dain, followed

by the other two elite angelics. To my utter dismay, they engaged Dain and the Trydentiums. The two sides fought each other mercilessly. Jr. and the two elites were winning! In a matter of moments, it turned. Dain and his brethren subdued the two Arqueiros and destroyed them. Dain overcame Jr.

I lunged to help Jr. and was unable to budge. I looked down and noticed the pinnacle had entangled my feet. Dain stood over Max Jr. with an evil grin, as the other Trydentiums surrounded him. *Whack!* Dain stomped on Maximino, as the other evil Trydentiums joined in, launching brutal attacks on Max Jr.

"No!" I yelled.

Enraged, my fists became ablaze with a blue fire. I waived my hand and called down electro birds from the sky. They swooped down and fired electric talons on the enemy. With a wave of my other hand, large cloud boulders came crashing down, engulfing Dain and all of the other Trydentiums.

*Whoa! I just did that?* I wondered.

I saw other angelics storm in to Jr.'s aid. It was the Lytenials! Max Jr. quickly recovered, striking back with his brethren.

*Kkkssssh!* Thunder rolled high in the sky to my left. It was so loud, it stunned me. I looked, and out of nowhere, an enormous black cloud, with black bolts of lightning, began to form.

High up in a cloud emerged a giant, black, gold-trimmed, transparent dragon. The massive dragon illuminated with radiance, with electric bolts surging around it, and red, beaming eyes. There was no mistaking who this beast was. This one, who brought great fear, trembling, and death, was the god, Lucio.

The beast let out a deafening roar that shook the foundation. Lucio breathed black fire and smoke that formed into the figures of all the lost souls he had devoured. The figures flew all around, screeching their unspeakable agony and suffering, and dissipated back into eternal torment. Lucio raised his arms, and suddenly smoke began seeping from cracks all over the ground, which spawned horrific demons.

I trembled in terror at the presence of such overwhelming power. Lucio, god of the world and darkness, instantly empowered the Trydentiums. Lucio transformed all of his dark offspring into mini-gods in their own right, making them larger and stronger as they illuminated with sheer energy.

They possessed the same powers as their Lytenial counterparts. They transformed into gods of wrath, pride, lust and gluttony. Others were gods of sexuality, envy, idolatry and witchcraft. Others were gods of slothfulness, drunkenness, hatred, murder, rebellion, suicide, and fear.

Dain, the god of fire, and god of all under-gods, specialized in morphing, and had the strength of all under-gods. He had beaming red eyes, and his body was ablaze with black fire, outlined in red fire. He was pure evil incarnate.

Lucio lit up, feeding energy of pure evil, which strengthened and empowered Dain and the Trydentiums. Max Jr. let out a fierce battle roar, standing his ground with his brethren behind him. Dain grinned and ordered the attack.

The Trydentiums attacked, striking the Lytenials mercilessly. It was too much, as Lytenials fell one by one to the overwhelming onslaught. Only Max Jr. was left standing, alone. Dain and all the demonic hoard of Trydentiums surrounded the mighty Mestre de Batalha.

*Oh no, I've seen this before. I'm not losing Jr. too.*

*Not today…*

I looked down at my bound feet and I did not accept it. A surge of maximum rage struck the core of my spirit. My entire body illuminated black, outlined with blue electricity. My eyes projected a white beam.

I leapt into the air and broke free. Like a bullet, I charged toward the Trydentiums, and was swiftly pummeled by Dain. He subdued me. Jr. reached to help me but couldn't. The superior Dain and the Trydentiums cheered and celebrated their victory, while chanting in their unknown tongue.

With a wicked grin, Dain looked back at his father, Lucio, for approval to complete his mission for me. Dain looked down and grabbed my arm to help me up and I felt something.

*Wind?* I thought, confused.

A familiar, gentle breeze hit my face. I looked up and saw a hat. The hat was floating in a gust of wind, and it rested on the ground in front of me.

It wasn't just any hat; it was a grey fedora with a white feather. A dove's feather. It was the signature unique hat of Jr.'s father. An instant reminder of what they've been telling me, A warm, tingling sensation covered my body, and I felt my spirit groan.

I looked up at the dumbfounded Dain, who now had large eyes.

While arm-in-arm, I said, "I chose wrong? No. You did!"

Instantly, I shot ultra-beams of white light into his eyes, blinding Dain. I grabbed Dain's other arm, and launched us both high into the air.

With no chance for Dain to recover, in a fit of ultimate rage and fury, I took Dain's arms and snapped them over my shoulder, breaking them. I followed with a crushing elbow to Dain's face, smashing it, and launched Dain into outer darkness. In that instant, I exhaled a flurry of wind spurted into the mouths and nostrils of the battered Lytenials, giving them instant life, and a burst of energy.

With no hesitation, I turned to Lucio and his horde of demonic Trydentiums. I charged the beast, and yelled in fury, "Mate ele!" which meant, "Kill him!"

The other Lytenials followed my lead. The beast god roared in a fit of great fury, knocking the Lytenials and me to the ground.

I was briefly knocked unconscious. I opened my eyes and

found myself lying on my back, underneath the enormous foot of Lucio.

I fought and struggled to break away. I couldn't. I gasped in horror.

Lucio lifted his foot over my head and—just as Lucio delivered my final blow—a beam of light shot out from the nearby woods. I looked, and it was him! Through the trees emerged Maximino Sr., with a glow of great splendor about him. Lucio, overwhelmed, stumbled back at the sight of such majestic radiance.

All stood in awe and disbelief. The mere presence of Max Sr. made the Trydentium demons cower. The great power and radiance displayed by Max Sr. was beyond comprehension. A burst of wind swept up the fedora hat, carrying it to the hand of Maximino Sr., who placed it on his head. Max Sr. crossed his arms and looked up at Lucio with a grin.

Lucio stepped up in a fit of rage, and roared in fury, exhaling a storm of black fire of lost souls so massive I couldn't see anything. The ground shook as legions of demons ascended on black clouds above, and from the pits below, a reminder of the sheer power and might of the god of death. The demons hissed and praised Lucio, rallying behind their god, ready for battle.

Suddenly, a thunderous crack in the sky was heard, piercing the ears of all. I saw the sky open, and a giant lighting cloud formed with deafening thunder. Out of the enormous cloud emerged an army of mighty angelic warriors. They covered the sky. They rode on chariots and horses of lightning and fire. The battle-hardened angelic Lytenials gleamed in radiant splendor and a ray of light beamed to all. The Trydentiums fell back.

The only one who remained standing was Lucio. Defiant until the bitter end, Lucio hissed, growled, and snapped his jaws at me. Lucio exhaled black fire and smoke, again releasing all the lost souls he devoured. Harrowing cries and screeches of great remorse were heard, as the lost souls cried and pleaded. The cloud that

EMBAIXADOR 185

carried me on top of the pinnacle suddenly carried me through the sky, toward the enraged giant beast god.

As the cloud carried me closer, I noticed the mighty dragon's scales began to fall apart, piece by piece. As I got closer, the fierce beast god became smaller, and smaller, as he continued to snap and lunge at me. Lucio's fire breathing became weaker, as the dragon's outer body dissipated to the core. As I came upon Lucio, it was only then, I realized, this was no fierce dragon, this was no mighty god. Before me now was a frail, old man, curled up on the ground, cowering in fear, begging me for mercy.

"You're the one who shook the earth? You're the one who deceived and plagued all of mankind, and turned all of humanity against itself? You killed my father, and hurt my little girl? It was you who destroyed my family!" I yelled.

All of a sudden, the ground underneath Lucio began to shake and bubble up, as if it were quicksand. Chains of mud and rock shot up from the ground, latching onto Lucio, entwining him. Lucio kicked, screamed, and clawed as he tried to break free.

Lucio shrieked and screamed in horror as he began to slowly sink. He tried to grasp for roots and rocks around him. Shoulder-deep, the old man looked into my eyes as he reached his hand out to me, and desperately cried out, "Please forgive… Help me. I'm sorry!"

The ground slowly began to swallow him. Lucio, the great beast, who had plagued mankind, was sinking into the same earth he corrupted.

The little god of death and darkness, who showed no mercy throughout his existence, had received none. Lucio was cast into the outer void. The remaining fallen dark angelics, the defected Trydentiums, began to shriek in horror as they sank into the earth, swallowed up into eternal damnation. Thunderous cheers and praises erupted from the massive angelic army that surrounded me.

The harrowing screeches continued from Lucio who was

devoured by the earth and defeated. The battle for me was won. I turned around and there, standing with me and Max Sr., Max Jr., and all of the Lytenials, were also my grandmother and grandfather, family and my friends who had completed their journey's. And all of them were in a mighty angelic form. That day, I saw people from every race and color. They were all now standing with me, side by side.

I recognized my other brothers with me there as well. I saw John and Enoch standing next to me, and over there were Peter and David. And there were Jacob, Elijah, and Job, smiling at me. By my side were all of the founding brethren who had paved the way for us from the beginning.

*Rel!* I thought. I was grieved and I looked around. Max Jr. walked up to me and nodded and smiled. I nodded back.

I was, side by side with the Lytenials and all my family. And yet I still felt as if something else were missing.

Suddenly, I heard, "My brother…"

I knew that voice. I turned and saw, my dad! Although I knew it was my dad, I didn't call him that. I placed my arm around his shoulder and I smiled, ear to ear. "My brother," I replied.

# 35
## LINE IN THE SAND

WHEN LUCIO, THE god of shadow, was gone, I was relieved it was over. I thought we had won. I was wrong. There were more than one. As we cheered and celebrated our victory over Lucio, an unsettling feeling hit me. I looked at the others around me and saw the looks of concern on the faces of the Lytenials.

Mighty strikes of the elements cracked through the sky. Wind, rain, hail, and lightning roared in the distance as a deep fear overcame me. There, not far away, in opposite directions, stood two other figures whom I also recognized before my time here on earth. It was the two Trydentium brother gods.

On one side stood Enlil, the god of command and destruction. And standing in the other direction was the creator Enki, the god of water. And with them came earthquakes, typhoons, tornadoes, and plagues, and swarms of pestilence of all kinds.

There they both stood with their minions and legions of demonic armies, and all of their dark glory as the sky above them turned dark and gray. The gods glared at each other, and then they turned to us with smirks on their faces. Instantly, my heart and spirit sank.

I felt a calm. An arm was felt around my shoulder. I looked up, and saw it was him! The one who drew the line in the world's sand first, Yeshua, Jesus the savior, our brother.

Suddenly, I heard piercing sounds of trumpets behind us. The elements and the legions of armies and plagues were instantly silenced. I turned around. Behind all of my family and friends, and every person, in the mist of the Lytenials, shot rays of gleaming light. A massive cloud appeared, with two giant angelic warriors, with eye-piercing resilience as they wielded in each hand blazing swords of fire. The two mighty angelics stood in front of the cloud, as if guarding it.

A blinding light shot from the cloud, and there emerged scores of angelic warriors like no other angelic. The mighty angelic army was so vast, it reached as far as the eye could see. And there, behind the mighty angelic warriors, with the dove of white hovering over his shoulder, was the God of gods.

Instantly, I felt a great peace. Every Lytenial, every animal, every plant and tree, and every living entity on the earth knelt before him. Thunderous, simultaneous praises were shouted so loudly it shook the earth.

I looked over at my God, who smiled and reached out his hand, and I took it, and I was called away home, to my father in heaven.

We all stood with God Almighty, as we faced the evil in front of us. My fists ignited flames and I let out a roar of fury to our enemies. Thunderous praises to our God were heard, deafening battle cries were shouted simultaneously, as we rallied behind our God.

I could not see through the bright rays of such majestic radiance, as I tried to look upon my God. My eyes could not contain the glory of his eyes. I did, however, see his form. And his skin, I saw, was changing. His skin slowly changed to all colors, continuously. He was the color of us all. I fell to my knees before my God, and worshiped him.

A deafening crack in the sky was heard as a blinding light projected from the omnipotent glory of God, which covered the earth.

I turned at everyone around me, and when I did, I was dumbfounded. I saw, there was no color. Race ceased to exist. We were all the same and all beliefs funneled into unity.

In an instant, there was total peace, as every person stood hand in hand. I saw the bond of every creature alike, as the lion now walked with the lamb.

Division was conquered here, for now.

Through the silence, I looked up, and there remained the two fallen Trydentium brother gods, Enlil and Enki, as they stood with their demonic forces, scowling. The two gods summoned their under-gods.

The under-gods from all sections of the earth came forward, with even more legions of evil hordes from the depths. And there, in the other direction stood the Ceifador, soul reaper war god, Nehriol. With him was Ceifeira, the reaper witch. They were impartial to the brother gods. They all glared at each other and turned to us. The claim to the world and to rule the gifts therein continued, as they stood, growling and hissing, ready for war.

Feeling a surge, within my spirit, we all joined as his sons and daughters together, and entered into our God, as one with the Alpha and the Omega.

All the Trydentium's, were left trembling in fear.

# 36

# NOT GOODBYE

"ALEB, HOLD UP. This is a very cool story and all, and thanks for getting back with me. But you're telling me it ends just like that? And what do you mean, you were called home to heaven? Are you saying you actually died and came back to life, only to tell me all of this now? You've got to be kidding me, man," Steven, my new friend said and laughed. He shook his head in disbelief, as he leaned down and petted my dog, Nalla.

Nalla's fur began to fall off with each pet. Nalla was a spirit.

"What the hell?" Steven said as he fell back. Steven, completely baffled, looked up at me. He was awestruck to see I was suddenly transparent, in a mighty angelic form with black transparent wings, trimmed with the white fire of an Arco de Batalha, a high arch angelic of hosts.

I replied, "No. Steven, I never died."

Shaking in fear, Steven reached out his hands in mercy and said, "Caleb?"

"Yes, it's me. Don't be afraid. Please, stand up."

A white dove arose from behind me, and hovered over my shoulder. Steven stood and was instantly at peace.

He looked around, realizing we were somewhere else.

"Where are we?"

"I brought you here, upon this pinnacle to show the conclusion to our story," I replied.

I told Steven the final battle I witnessed here, upon the pinnacle, wasn't a battle for me. It was a battle for him. I represented all of us that day. I was you.

And, as Rel, Maximino Sr., Max Jr., and all the Montez brothers and sisters watched over me, they were also watching over you.

It was them, Steven, the Lytenials, who have been with you, guiding and protecting you from the beginning, guarding the gifts within you and all of us, every day, all over the world.

Even now, in this foreign land, the fight continues against the Trydentiums, the seekers of the shadow, filling their own with darkness and death, as they seek to destroy the gifts in us all.

And, although the battle for me was won and I was called home, never to have experienced a natural death, the fight here for you, the only battle that matters, continues.

I told Steven that as I was on the pinnacle that overlooked the final battle, I was also shown something. The cloud that carried me on top of this pinnacle completely engulfed me. Inside the cloud, I was shown every moment I'd spent on this earth. It was a life I once called a waste, convinced it would have been better had I not been born. If only I knew how wrong I was.

I lost my focus as a father, a husband and family man to everything else.

I was determined to be better than my neighbors, co-workers, friends, and family, and I had to be the first to get it. If I desired an item, food, or woman, I was going to have it. And I schemed and lied to get whatever it was. All at the cost of hurting others, and losing my precious family.

My reward was to have my name mentioned, and get the praises of others, a pat on the back, and a fully satisfied ego to blanket my own insecurities. I truly missed this mark.

My purpose here, this life, wasn't to obtain great wealth, material things, or overindulgences, as I had always been taught. Nor was it about being the smartest or the fastest, the strongest or the fittest. Being tall or skinny or popular never had anything to do with it. It was never about that, or me; it was all a mirage.

Inside the cloud, I discovered the more I took, the less I had in the end. My legacy, which I had built my entire life here, never was. I looked down at my two hands, these very hands I'd put to work so hard for me, and I reflected on what I have done with them and I found them empty. It was never about taking, but to give.

Now, I know what the reason for life is. It's so, we can give it.

This beautiful and unique gift, given only to me in all of creation, breathed by God. And throughout my journey here, every person I talked to, every hand I shook, and anyone's eyes I looked into, who saw my gift, also received it. I realized I was reenergizing others with this gift since my first step.

Every day, my life played a crucial role in helping others, so they could do the same in return.

And the path I blazed here was only because of the direction and choice I made in that grey wasteland.

It was Rel, my first guardian angel, who told me the right way from the beginning. Now I know what Rel was referring to when he told me, that day, that I was on the way back. I traveled back home, to my roots.

I challenged and called on this God to show himself to me, and he answered. This God I searched for, and sought outwardly, was always within me. It wasn't God who hurt my daughter, nor did he take everything away from me. He never took my dad; my dad has given his gift and his mission was complete. And now, it's this gift Steven, I give to you.

Steven held his head low knowing what that meant.

I also told him, all of my human errors, my flaws, and my many shameful mistakes, were all absorbed with this gift. Everywhere I went, and everyone I encountered, I was guarded. At my lowest and darkest times, even as I tried to end it all, I was never alone. Everyone, from the heavyset woman speaking gibberish at the post office, to Que, the nurse at the hospital, the little native Lipan Apache boy, and Max Jr. were all purposely placed in my path.

I was unknowingly entertaining my angelic brothers and sisters, the Lytenials, all along. In another realm, they had been relentlessly fighting the darkness of the Trydentiums behind the scenes. It was they who guided me, with subtle words and simple misdirection to ensure I was safe, and I remained heading in the direction that only I was sent to travel.

While in the cloud, I also saw the article I had always laughed at. It was the story of the toddler who fell out of a twelve-story window. I discover that the toddler was me. And it was Rel, my original guardian angel, who caught me. This was something my father always knew.

I told Steven there was one last thing I saw on this pinnacle. I was immediately taken back as a young boy, as I walked back from the corner store with my dad. I was so happy to relive that moment again. I could feel my dad's hand as I held it tight, while eating a push-up ice cream in the other hand.

I recalled that when I looked up at my dad, I was only able to see his partial smile through the bright sunlight.

This time, I saw something more. As I looked up, the sunlight began to fade away, and I noticed there was someone else there with us that day. Confused, I looked up at my dad, who smiled and nodded as he patted my head. My dad then turned to the other person and smiled.

I looked, and there walking with us next to my dad, was Max's father, Maximino Sr., with his gray trademark fedora hat with a dove's feather. Max Sr. gave a nod to my father., He smiled and gave me a wink. Max Sr. then turned and waved at another small boy, who was sitting on the steps next to us as we walked by.

That little boy, Steven, was you. It was your father's barber shop we would always pass every week. That day, you were sitting on the front steps, eating your ice cream, as you smiled and waved back.

Now I know why both of our dads would always smile and wave at each other. They knew as we passed, we strengthened and filled each other.

In the end, when the meaning of faith finally became real to me, everything reset. I no longer needed to see these things naturally. I have felt and seen from within. This is what has decided the outcome of my battle for my mission.

After my journey here, I looked down with my father from above, just as in my vision, and upon the oil rig, I could again see everything. I saw Tiana holding my little girl, Taylor, crying as she mourned my parting. Tiana reflected all the memories we shared together during my time here, and the positive mark I left behind. She was greatly saddened. For the first time since the car accident, I heard my little girl suddenly speak.

"It's okay, Momma, I saw Daddy go to heaven on a cloud, just like he told me," Taylor said.

Shocked, Tiana screamed in happiness, as tears of hurt and sorrow turned to joy. She replied, "Yes, honey, that's right. That's right." She held her tight, and thanked God.

That's when I saw my heavenly Father motion with his hand, and sent a friend to them, a dove. Instantly, they were at peace and my little Taylor's arm was healed and she hugged Tiana. Taylor hugged Tiana in her arms.

Tiana headed over to my mother's, and told her of this miracle. Tiana also revealed to my mother another miracle. Tiana told my mother she was pregnant with my son, Caleb Jr. I looked at my mother and she looked up at me and smiled. They grieved no more. They understood my journey here was finished, and now their journey with Taylor and my son, carry's on.

With watery eyes, Steven asked, "So you're leaving? This is goodbye?" I replied, "Not goodbye. Even though our assignment here is finished, another is assigned after."

I told Steven that the two brother gods, both of them determined to take claim to the world, remained, as their time was not yet.

And, throughout the darkness that surrounds us every day, no matter what may be going on around us here in this world, know that the Lytenials, guardians of light and truth, our brethren, are with you, always.

As long as our friend, this dove of white, remains here, the spirit of peace and protection will follow.

We will continue our fight, to protect the only thing here that matters, the precious gift that has been given to us, the gift of life.

I felt a surge through Steven Riley's spirit. He looked up with a fire in eyes and his fists grew large and began to light up.

"The pain you carry, to all who hurt and suffer, and to those who are left feeling empty and abandoned, I have been sent here to bring this message: I'm Caleb John McCray from the Lytenial tree-line, Embaixador from my Father in heaven, and you are not alone. Throughout this journey, until each one of our mission here completes, we will all have a story to tell.

This was my story. What will be yours?"

# Epilogue

*"It was the day I discovered it, and I will tell it ..."*

- STEVEN RILEY

*"Be not forgetful to entertain strangers: for thereby
some have entertained angles unawares."*

-HEBREWS 13:2

# Acknowledgments

To the loves of my life, my children Kyra, Kalynn, Camden, Marcus Jaden, and Brenden, thank you for never giving up on me. My parents Marcus and Katherine, who instilled in me to believe all things are possible. To my brother Jason, and my sister Kristen "Sauce Queen" who has always reminded me of who I really am when I would forget. My late great grandfather John Frank, my "Avô" who also inspired this story. Last but not least Emily, who never let me put the pen down. Thank you all. During the many dips and valleys in the journey of this book, it was the love and belief of all my family and friends throughout the years which has given me the strength to ignite the flame, which is inside us all, to accomplish my dream.

And, thanks again to my family and friends for allowing me to portray them in this story. Trust me, Caleb thanks you too.

Kids... Daddy really did it, finally. = D

# From the Author

Throughout life I realized most of the time, we focus on the negative image painted around us. Although, initially we feel to act on the negative, I found it was the positive to have the greater impact. This changed my perception on everything and even those around me, so I was determined to portray exactly that through- out my travels and in this writing.

-Even the smallest positive gesture in a world surrounded in darkness, will always reflect a light.

No matter our differences in views or beliefs, no matter how our perception may be in this world, no one can deny the value and impact of our lives to each other. I hope this reminder and message of this story has brought as much joy as I have found in writing it.

-Do what you know to do at this exact moment that will get you on the right path going forward.

Stay the path. -Marcus John

Marcus John Beltran, best known as a father of five. He was born in 29 palms, Marine Corps base and raised in Point Loma, CA. and now resides in Fort Worth, TX. Prior to his debut novel, *Embaixador*, he was a banking analyst, he also was actively involved in a young adult focus group encouraging others to awaken the passion and divinity within. A devoted father by day and creator by night. Currently, he's turning the page, to the next chapter, of life.

# GLOSSARY

Embaixador: A Portuguese word for ambassador.

Ambassador: An important individual from a foreign land representing his or her own land, and who is officially accepted in this position by that land.

# INDEX

LYTENIALS™

TRYDENTIUMS™